WAITING IN DARKNESS

A SABRINA VAUGHN NOVEL

MAEGAN BEAUMONT

PRAISE OF THE SABRINA VAUGHN SERIES

"Prepare to be overwhelmed by the tension and moodiness that permeates this edgy thriller. Beaumont's ability to keep the twists coming even when the answer seems obvious is quite potent."
—*LIBRARY JOURNAL*

"Pulse-pounding terror, graphic violence and a loathsome killer."
—*KIRKUS REVIEWS*

"Beaumont knows how to keep you on the edge of your seat...Buckle up for the ride of a lifetime." —*SUSPENSE MAGAZINE*

"...twists and turns along the way that kept me guessing until the very end."—**OPENBOOKSOCIETY.COM**

"Beaumont knows how to cook up and serve a dish called revenge, but she doesn't serve it cold. She serves it sizzling hot."—**Vincent Zandri, best-selling author of** *THE REMAINS*

Edge-of-the-seat plotting will keep readers' attention late into the night."—*LIBRARY JOURNAL*

"Reads like the transcript of a breathlessly bloody computer game."—*PUBLISHERS WEEKLY* "Intricately developed plots, higher stakes, and unlikely criminals that astonish by executing twist after unforeseeable twist."—Ava Black, *CRIMESPREE MAGAZINE*

"Maegan Beaumont knows exactly what the reader wants and tantalises them with her seductive writing style until nothing else matters except devouring the story." - **BOOKCHATTER BLOG**

"Maegan Beaumont has crafted a superb thriller!"—**Les Edgerton, acclaimed author of** *THE BITCH* **and** *JUST LIKE THAT*

THE SABRINA VAUGHN SERIES

WAITING IN DARKNESS

CARVED IN DARKNESS

SACRIFICIAL MUSE

PROMISES TO KEEP

BLOOD OF SAINTS

(Available August, 2016 by Midnight Ink)

AUTHOR'S NOTE

A lot of people have asked me, *Why a prequel? Why now?* The answer, like the question, is twofold. The first—*why a prequel?*—is fairly simple. This novel has always existed. When I wrote the first draft of *Carved in Darkness*, I incorporated an alternate timeline, telling Melissa's story alongside Sabrina's, weaving it into the present-day story. The problem was that the original version of that novel was 750 pages long. Even as untried and inexperienced as I was, I knew that a 750 page novel from an unknown author would never get published. So, I killed my darlings. And it hurt. So much so that I never stopped thinking about it, which eventually led us here.

The second—*why now?*—all comes down to timing. The fourth novel in the Sabrina Vaughn series, *Blood of Saints*, takes her back to the place where she was abducted and held—Yuma, Arizona—and I wanted the opportunity to introduce readers to the people and places in the story beforehand because they're important to me. If you're a first time reader, I hope you enjoy the story enough to continue on and if you've been a reader from the beginning, I hope I've done right by you, because in the end, to me, that's all that really matters.

For *you.*
Thanks for sticking with me.

ONE

Jessup, Texas
April ~ 1998

"MELISSA JEAN, I SWEAR that kid's gonna stare a hole right through your ass," Terry muttered under her breath as she took a blueberry pie from the glass display case on the lunch counter. "I don't know how you stand it." She cut a generous wedge to place on a plate for the trucker at table six.

Throwing a cautious glance over her shoulder, Melissa's eyes flitted over Jed Carson. He was staring at her again. Hiding her discomfort behind a polite smile, she forced herself not to look away when his gaze traveled upward to meet her own.

He didn't smile back.

Turning, she focused her attention on the task of filling the huge, commercial-sized coffee maker with water. "As long as he stays on his side of the counter and pays his bill before he leaves, he can stare all he wants," she said. Truth was, she wished he'd leave. Not just the diner. She wished he'd leave Jessup for good and never come back.

"He ain't going anywhere." Terri shot another glare his way. "How many times have you re-filled his coffee cup?"

Ten. She'd counted. Every time she did he used the opportunity to try and talk to her. Ask her about her grandmother. Her mom. Her brother and sister. Like he cared about any of them at all. Like he cared about her. He didn't care about her. He wanted to sleep with her. Even at sixteen, she knew the difference. "I don't know," she said. "One time or fifty, doesn't matter."

"Which makes him no different from the rest of the losers around here," Tommy said from the service window, a plate in his hand. "Your boyfriend's order is up," he said, nudging it toward her with that asshole smirk of his that made her want to slap the eyeballs right out of his head.

"He's *not* my boyfriend." She hissed back, shooting him a glare.

"Does he know that?" Tommy countered dryly, turning toward the flat grill to work over a couple of eggs and a slab of bacon for the trucker at table six.

She snatched the plate off the counter. "I hate you sometimes."

"Good," he shot back without looked at her. His tone was hard, like he meant it and she immediately wanted to apologize. Instead, she turned and walked down the length of the counter to where Jed'd parked himself and delivered his food.

"You think I could get a little..." Jed's words died out as she set the double bacon and cheese with a side of fries in front of him and without a word, pulled a bottle of steak sauce from her apron pocket and set it down in front of his plate.

"Well, look at me, forgettin' I got the best damn waitress in Texas," he said, smiling at her. She was sure that any other girl in town would've fainted dead away if Jed had looked at them the way he looked at her. With his sandy blonde hair and soft hazel eyes, he was easily the best looking boy in Jessup. He was captain of the varsity football team, Homecoming king and senior class president. All of this and for some reason he wanted *her*—and she wasn't the slightest bit interested.

"A re-fill on the coffee'd be most appreciated, Melissa Jean," Jed said, leaning toward her just a bit. He did it every time she poured and it'd taken her a while to figure out why. He was smelling her. She could hear his deep intake of breath near her ear when she bent her head to fill his cup.

Plastering that vague, polite smile on her face, she pretended not to notice. She also pretended not to notice the flask he slipped out of the pocket of his letterman's jacket or that he added a healthy dose of whiskey to the brew. He had been drinking for the past hour, steadily moving toward drunk with every re-fill.

"You get off in an hour. Wanna do something?" Jed said, watching her over the rim of his cup. The burger and fries would go untouched. Just another excuse to talk to her.

"I can't. Gotta get home." Her answer was always the same. She never said yes to him but he seemed hurt and confused by her rejection every time.

"It's Friday night," he said carelessly, like someone who'd never shouldered a responsibility in his life.

"Sure is," she said. "Which means I got to be back here at 7AM."

Jed shook his head, not buying it. "Why do you always say no to me, Melissa? What? I got an ear growin' out the middle of my forehead or somethin'? " Leaning back from the counter like a sullen child, Jed folded his arms across his chest and glared at her with an insolent pout, better suited for a boy of five rather than eighteen.

"No, what you've got is a girlfriend and she ain't me. Where is Shelly anyway?" Throwing his girlfriend into the mix usually worked at getting him to back off but not tonight. The whiskey in his system made him stubborn and she knew from past experience, mean.

"I'm not with her cause she ain't who I want to be with." He shot her that winning smile again. "Come on; just let me give you a ride home, what's the harm in that?"

Plenty. She formed another rejection in her mind, ready to temper it with one of her many excuses but before she could get it out, the bell above the diner door gave a tinkle and Wade Bauer strolled in.

"I knew I'd find you here," he said, adding a friendly smile as he approached the counter. "Hey, Melissa, how's things?"

"They're fine," she said, barely able to suppress the groan of relief that welled up in her throat. Jed and Wade were nearly inseparable. If anyone could get him up and out of her hair, it was him.

Throwing her a sympathetic smile behind Jed's back, Wade sat on the edge of the neighboring stool and gave his friend a nudge with his foot. "Pay the girl and let's go. We're all hangin' at Duffy's house."

"I'm busy," Jed said, his eyes glued to her face.

Wade gave her a nervous glance. Sometimes she got the feeling that Jed's fixation on her made him uncomfortable. He rubbed the back of his neck and tried again. "Come on, man. Shelly's waitin' on you. Been asking for you all night."

Jed made disgusted sound in the back of his throat. "I bet she has."

"So, let's git before the rest of the guys drain the keg and your girl still has time to get busy before she's gotta make curfew," Wade said, clapping a hand on Jed's shoulder to urge him along.

"I got an idea—how about *you* go fuck Shelley." Jed shrugged Wade's hand away and lifted his cup to his mouth, taking a long swallow before he spoke again. "Because I ain't goin' nowhere."

Wade cut her a look, quick and sharp. "Come on, man—"

"I s*aid* I ain't leavin'—not without my peach pie," Jed said, letting his gaze fall, heavy and full of meaning, on Melissa's face.

His words burned red circles on her cheeks and she reached for the coffee pot again, looking for any excuse to move, to disguise the nervous flutter of her hands. "Coffee, Wade?" she said, avoiding Jed's eyes which were boring holes into her face.

"No thanks—one cup of coffee and the four beers I drank on the way here are wasted," he said, laughing as he reached across the counter and gave her thick auburn ponytail a playful tug. He was trying to keep things light but she could tell he was struggling. "Tell you what, hack off a piece of pie for the peach lover here, throw it in a doggy bag and I'll drag his ass out of here for you." His mouth grinned at her but his eyes told a different story entirely. He felt just as uncomfortable as she did.

Ignoring Wade, Jed continued to glare at her, his arms crossed stubbornly over his chest. "What about the half-breed back there? He like peach pie?"

Dread dropped into her gut like a stone. "Jed, please don't—"

Suddenly he was shoving himself away from the counter and standing, the whiskey he'd been drinking and the sudden movement sending him swaying on his feet. "Hey, Tomahawk," he shouted. "You like peach pie?"

Looking around nervously, Melissa noted that Terry was gone—probably stepped out back to smoke—and with the exception of a few over the road haulers, and the trucker at table six, the only other person in the diner was a man who was vaguely familiar, sitting at a booth in the back, near the waitress station. He watched the exchange openly, the paperback he had open in front of him completely forgotten, his eyes, dark and unreadable, zeroed in on her. Melissa felt a ripple of unease but it lasted only seconds before she looked away.

Like he'd been waiting, Tommy pushed his way through the swinging door connecting the kitchen to the service area behind the counter, wiping his hands on a dish towel on his way.

"I think Wade's right," Tommy said, coming to stand beside her. "It's time the two of you head out." Shifting his weight, he leaned against her and with the slightest nudge of his arm against her own, moved her behind him in a protective gesture that was unmistakable. Melissa threw a brief look over her shoulder. The young man in the back booth wasn't sitting anymore. He was standing, book tossed on the table, watching the exchange. Waiting.

"Oh... is that what you think?" Tommy's movement grabbed Jed's attention. He zeroed in on him with narrowed eyes. "You think just because your uncle owns this pile of shit and calls it a restaurant, you actually mean somethin'?" Jed said, his tone just as nasty as his glare. Suddenly, that glare slid toward her and shifted into something else. Something that made her feel dirty. "You still haven't answered my question, Tomahawk—you like peach pie?"

"Get him out of here," Tommy said to Wade, ignoring Jed completely.

Watching the scene play out over Tommy's shoulder, Melissa saw the way Wade studied him beneath the curly tangle of light brown hair that fell across his forehead. If a punch was thrown, Wade would undoubtedly enter the fray and it would become two against one. Waiting to see if Wade would decide to play peacemaker or hold Tommy down while Jed threw the punches, Melissa tried to move out from behind Tommy but was sufficiently blocked— his broad, solid back pushed against her, telling her to stay put.

Just when the confrontation seemed to be on the brink of inevitable violence, Wade aimed his gaze past them for a moment. What he saw seemed to make up his mind and he stepped forward, an easy smile aimed her way.

"Now ain't the time," he said in a low tone, dropping a hand on Jed's shoulder before pulling him away from the counter with a laugh. "If you plan on gettin' any tonight you better hurry—Shelley's curfew's in a few hours," he said, deciding to play the peacemaker after all.

"Yeah... I bet you *looove* you some peach pie, don't you, half-breed?" Stepping back from the counter, Jed shrugged into his jacket. "You ain't shit, Onewolf," he said, baring his teeth in a vicious smile. "You ain't never gonna have nothin' or be nothin' just like your dead injun' daddy," he called out in a taunting voice, still trying, even as he was being pulled out the door by Wade, to bait Tommy into a fight.

Tommy's muscles bunched beneath the thin cotton of his shirt as he readied himself to vault across the counter after Jed. Without thinking, she reached out and laid her hands on his back, silently urging him to resist the bait Jed was dangling.

"See you 'round, Melissa," Jed said before being pushed through the door and into the parking lot. A few minutes later Jed's shiny red convertible sped out of the parking lot, spraying dirt and gravel against the plate glass of the diner window, Wade's pick-up close behind.

Weak with relief, Melissa laid her cheek against Tommy's shoulder and let her eyes slip shut. He stood stalk still, arms hanging loose at his sides with hands that clenched themselves into fists as he stared out the wide window of the diner. "Don't," he said to her, the word slipping past teeth that were clenched too tight and she instantly remembered who and where she was. "Not here."

"Sorry," she said, dropping her hands away from his back, stepping away from him.

"I'm walking you home," he said without looking at her, almost like he was talking to someone else.

Glancing at her watch, Melissa saw that it was just past nine o'clock. She had 45 minutes left on her shift but the diner didn't close until midnight. "You don't have to— they're not coming back," she said, retying her apron to give her hands something to do. "Besides, I can't wait that long—I gotta get the twins from Mrs. Kirkland's in an hour."

Moving from behind the counter, Tommy walked toward the diner's double glass doors and flipped the sign to CLOSED.

"Tommy, your uncle is gonna blow a gasket if he comes by and sees you closed up three hours early," she said as he moved past her toward the kitchen.

"I'm walking you home," he said again and his tone left no room for argument.

TWO

IT TOOK NEARLY A half hour to clear the rest of the customers out of the diner. Feeling bad, Melissa placed slabs of pie into Styrofoam containers while Terri filled large to-go cup with coffee and sent each customer off with an apologetic smile and dessert on the house.

The last to leave was the young man in the back booth. "I thought that was you." Tommy cut him a grin while he worked the cash register and counted out change. "When did you get back, O'Shea?" he said, dropping a handful of change and a few bills into the guy's hand.

As soon as she heard the name, Melissa recognized the face. Michael O'Shea. He looked different than she remembered. His hair was short—military short—no longer lank and long against his neck. His face was different too. He looked clean. Healthy.

He caught her looking, pinning her with a set of dark gray eyes, the corner of his mouth tipped up in a lopsided grin and she remembered who he was and has he'd done. The trouble and pain he'd caused. That he'd abandoned his little sister after his parents died and she looked away from him, suddenly wishing him gone.

As soon as she looked away he aimed his attention toward Tommy and answered his question. "Yesterday. They gave me a few weeks leave before I start Ranger school," he said with a shrug. "The old man finally got rid of it, huh?" he said, jerking his chin at the place where an old, freestanding video game used to be.

Tommy followed his gaze and laughed. "Yeah, it must've died of loneliness because it stopped working right after you left."

Michael must've found it amusing that something in Jessup had actually missed him because he laughed too.

"Here," she said, shoving a container full of pie into his hands. "Not sure what kind it is."

Taking the container, Michael lifted the lid and took a peek. "Peach," he said, looking at her, another lopsided grin plastered across his face. "My favorite."

Before she could form a response he dropped the change Tommy had given him into her outstretched hand. "Give that to Terri, will ya?" He turned away before she could answer. "See ya around, Onewolf," he said over his shoulder and then he was gone.

TWENTY minutes later the diner was closed up and she and Tommy headed toward the park, cutting through it toward home—a rickety single-wide with cardboard over the windows and a front porch that was really nothing more than a sheet of plywood and a few stacks of cinder blocks. On impulse, Melissa grabbed his hand, lacing her fingers between his and he instantly stiffened.

"Melissa," he said, trying to untangle his hand from hers. "Someone might—"

"Someone might *what?*" she said, using her other hand to gesture down the dark, deserted path they were traveling. "See us? I got news for you Tommy—I'm Kelly Walker's daughter. No one cares much about what the town whore's daughter does or who she does it with."

"You're a hell of a lot more than that and you know it." Tommy scowled at her. He hated it when she talked about herself like that. "If your father finds out we're together, he'll string me up."

Her father. The thought of him soured her belly and for a moment she had the urge to let go of Tommy's hand. Instead she tightened her grip. "No, he won't— because that would come too close to claiming me for Chief Bauer's comfort."

"He's not the only person around here who'd have a problem with a white girl dating an Indian," Tommy said, shaking his head at her.

She knew he was right. Jessup was a small town. People here were still closed-minded and judgmental about things like that. "I don't care what he thinks or anyone else for that matter."

"That's not true and we both know it." He was right about that too—she did care. She wanted people to look at her and see something better than who and where she'd come from. Just once, she'd like to hear her father say her name out loud. "I *don't* care," she said, her voice going wobbly. "He's never given me a reason to."

"Your father," he said gruffly. "Is that why you're doing this with me? To get back at him?"

This. Like what they had together was just a thing. Like it didn't matter.

She looked down at where they were joined—their fingers woven together. Hers tightly wrapped. His loose, ready to let her go at a moment's notice. For some reason, it made her angry. She let go and started walking. "Why do you keep doing this, Tommy? Why can't you just let things be good between us?"

"Because I'm never gonna drive a convertible and I'm never gonna go to college." He kept pace with her as he shook his head, giving her a sad look. "I'm gonna work at that goddamned diner until the day I die and you deserve better than that."

"Jed." She stopped walking. Turning, she stared at him, her ears ringing like he'd slapped her. "This is about Jed?"

"It's about all of them." He ran a hand through his hair, letting out a frustrated sigh. "About how almost every guy in this goddamned town would be better for you than me. But sure, we'll start with Jed—peach pie?"

Peach pie. The words were like a fist to her gut, nearly knocking the wind out of her. "I don't understand," she said quietly, even though she understood perfectly.

20

"Yes you do." Tommy shook his head, refusing to buy the act. "What was he talking about?"

The moment he said it, a flush crept up her neck—hot and splotchy—to settle against her cheeks. "Who knows?" she shrugged, looking away, using the dark to hide the truth. She'd always been a terrible liar. "He was drunk, talking nonsense."

Tommy was unconvinced. "Are you seeing him?"

"What?" The questions stung.

"Look—I understand if you are," he said, reaching for her hand, he smoothed a work-callused thumb over the newly heal burn on the back of it. "He's—"

"You don't understand anything." She yanked her hand back. Tears stung her eyes and she had to take a few deep breaths to steady herself before she spoke. "This is what he wanted. Why he said what he did. To make you angry. To make you think things that aren't true," she said quietly, shaking her head. "You're letting Jed win."

"Something happened between you two," Tommy said, frowning. "And I want to know what."

She sighed. "Why does it matter?"

"*Because,*" he yelled, the boom of his voice bouncing off the trees that surrounded them. He stopped and took a deep breath. "Because," he started again in a quieter voice. "I don't understand what... why *you* want to be with *me*. I got nothing—not a damn thing to offer you."

"Offer me?" she said it quietly. "Like money? Like I'm some kinda whore? Like my mother."

"That's not what..." The tables had suddenly turned and he sighed, rubbing his free hand across his forehead like he was dizzy. "That's not what I meant."

"Then what did you mean?" she said, her voice gaining an edge she'd always been careful to dull before. "Why wouldn't I want to be with you? Because of this?"

She pointed at her face. Like she was looking in a mirror, she could see it. The delicate arch of cheekbones that swept into a lush fall of auburn hair. Wide blue eyes set over the perfect slope of her nose. The generous set of her mouth above a flawlessly angled chin. Even her ears were perfect. Melissa hated it. She hated all of it.

Every time she saw herself, she saw her mother and she felt sick. "Is this all there is to me?"

"What? No." He looked at her like she'd spit on him but she'd seen it, the guilt that flashed in his eyes before he looked away from her.

She looked down at her hand. The starburst scar still pink and shiny. She'd gotten it a few weeks ago when she'd been helping him in the kitchen at the diner. For what felt like the hundredth time, she wished it was on her face. "Do you love me?" she said, looking up at him.

He stood there, staring at her—the sharp angles of his face thrown into deep shadow, the dark irises of his eyes glimmering silver in the moonlight. "You know I do," he said, sounding almost helpless.

"Why?" It was a question she'd never asked before. One she was afraid of. "Why do you love me?"

His mouth clamped shut, the look of helplessness that sat on his face twisting into one of confusion. He looked away from her, like he was trying to find an answer that would satisfy them both.

She waited, each seconds' worth of silence that ticked away, ringing in her ears. Finally she nodded, offering him a small smile. "Goodnight, Tommy," she said, her chin tipped up to keep it from trembling.

She walked away and he let her.

THREE

HE FOLLOWED HER HOME.

He'd been doing it for a while now—showing up at the diner right around closing and then hanging around the parking lot until she and that cocksucker fry cook locked up and left for the night. They'd usually part ways—she'd walk through the park while he cut across Main. This time, Onewolf walked with her.

They were real careful in public. Never touched. Never let themselves look at each other longer than a moment or two. They barely said two words to each other most nights. But he'd seen it. The way he'd come charging out of the kitchen to defend her. The way he'd pushed her behind him to protect her. It was obvious to anyone with a pair of eyes and half a brain, what was going on between them.

Lucky for them Jessup was full of half-retarded idiots.

He didn't like it. Decided, then and there, that he was going to do something about it. She was going to remember who she belong to. He'd make sure of that.

Needing to feel her—*smell her*—his hand strayed to the pocket of his jacket but he stopped himself from reaching inside.

Not here. Not yet.

Reaching into his other pocket, he ran his fingertips along the hilt of the large folding K-BAR he kept there. The handle was a bit worn from use, his fingers fitting into the grooves they'd made over the years. How many things had he killed with it? How much blood had cooled against its blade? More things than he could remember. More blood than he wanted to forget.

But never a person. Not yet.

He'd decided, the moment that filthy half-breed put his hands on her, that his would be the first human belly he'd stick his knife into. Tommy Onewolf was gonna look at him and *know* that he'd put hands on something that didn't belong to him.

He kept off the cement path they walked down, sticking to the trees, slipping from shadow to shadow, close enough to hear their conversation. They were fighting. He accused her of cheating on him and she denied it, turning the tables on him. "Why?" he heard her say. "Why do love me?"

He knew the answer. He knew why he loved her. Known since the first time he'd ever laid eyes on her. She'd been nothing but a girl then but he'd seen it, lurking in the impossible blue of her eyes. The truth. She belonged to him. The word wadded in his belly, tight and hard, like a rock.

Mine.

That one word played on a constant loop in his head whenever he saw her. Taunting him. Driving him crazy with its insistent drone. In it, he felt an impossible weight bearing down on him. A need he'd been fighting for as long as he could remember.

He wanted to do things to her. Bad things. Things that, once they were done, he would not be able to undo. Every second of every day, those things pushed at him, hardening from want to need.

Someday soon he'd give in to them. Instead of scaring him, those things he wanted to do excited him. His hand begin to wander again. He had to clench it into a fist to keep it from reaching into his pocket.

Not here. Not yet.

He heard her say goodnight to Onewolf. Watched her continue on toward home on her own. Knowing her routine, he waited, watching as she entered the trailer park. She veered left, toward the nicer, well-lit side of the park. This was where the old woman who watched her siblings lived. As soon as Melissa disappeared, he crossed the street, heading for the thick line of trees that divided the trailer park in two, he kept his head down, the dark ball cap he wore tugged low on his head until the trees swallowed him. People knew him. If someone saw him, they'd give him a puzzled smile and try to make conversation. Nosing in. Trying to figure out what he was doing here.

He walked, heading for the back of the property, the tree-line thickening as he went. When he reached the very end, he turned right and walked a bit further until he saw the dim outline of the rusted-out trailer she lived in. Every light in the place was on except hers. He waited outside her window, hidden in the trees. She would be home soon.

Unable to wait any longer, he reached into his jacket pocket, his hand eagerly closing over the pair of cotton panties he'd stolen from her room a few days ago. He rubbed them between his thumb and forefinger, the scalloped lace that skirted their hem scraped against his fingers.

He'd watched her take them off. Could still feel the heat of her trapped in the thin fabric where they'd fit between her legs. She'd slipped them off her gently rounded hips. Pulled them down her long, slim legs. He held them up to his face and breathed deep. Taking in the dark, secret smell of her. She'd be home soon. She'd know he was there. That he was waiting for her in the dark...

She smiled at him, crooking her finger. Beckoning him. Inviting him inside and he'd go to her. Climb inside her window...

One hand gripped the wad of cotton while the other fumbled with the fly of his jeans. He yanked them open and freed himself, cool April air caressing his exposed flesh. He wrapped the panties around his cock, closing his hand around them both. Working his fist up and down— his fingers tightening and releasing on every slide, covering himself with her scent.

She was on the bed, wearing nothing but a pair of white cotton panties. Legs spread wide, waiting for him with her eyes closed, fingers skimming over the crotch of her underwear, lips parted in a soft, eager moan. She wanted him. What he was going to do to her. She'd been waiting her whole life for it, just like him. He stood at the edge of the bed, between her open legs, taking off his shirt. His belt. His shoes. His pants.

And then he drew his knife, working the blade free from its handle with a whispering snick *that stilled the hand between her thighs and pulled her eyes open.*

That's when she saw him. The real him.

She tried to twist away, but he was already there, on top of her, pressing himself into the space her fingers had made wet for him. He'd kiss her and she'd pull back, her lush auburn hair slung across her face. Her mouth open, her chest heaving against his, filling her lungs with air, readying to scream.

He lifted the knife and she went still as he pressed it against the curve of her breast. Deep, blue eyes wide and stark with fear, her breath racing from her lungs in short, panicked bursts, each one pushing her breast against his blade.

He cut her—the edge of his blade whispering across her skin as he pushed himself inside her, the pain and blood of both, sharpening her fear into terror...

He was so engrossed in the scenario inside his head that he didn't see her at first but suddenly she was there. He could see the silhouette of her through the filter of thin fabric that covered her window.

She locked her bedroom door and began to undress, slow hands reaching behind her to untie her apron. Tired fingers fumbling the buttons of her yellow dress open before letting it slip from her shoulders. Next she unhooked her bra…

The hand between his legs worked faster, his hips swinging forward, matching the uneven rhythm of his breath as it broke from his mouth in a single whispered word, over and over.

Mine. Mine. Mine…

Fantasy and reality began to blur and the image of her in his head and the one in front of him merged. Became one in a violent smear of blood and sex. He came, the hand on his cock tightening and jerking around the head of it, catching his semen in the folds of white cotton, while his hips bucked and his teeth clamped down, holding in the sound of his release.

When it was over he put himself away. The light in her window went dark and he left, the smell of them together—her sex mingled with his—still riding on his skin.

FOUR

THE TRUCKER FROM TABLE six was sitting in her living room.

He'd been there when she woke up, bringing the twins into the kitchen to feed them breakfast. She'd noticed him instantly, her gaze jerking away the moment it touched on him to focus on the buckle of her sister's highchair rather than the fact that his attention snapped at her the moment she walked into the room.

Like he'd been waiting for her.

Riley looked up at her, her bright copper curls bouncing as she banged the flat of her chubby hand against her highchair tray. "Morning, baby," she said quietly, offering the toddler a tight smile. She didn't know the difference. As soon as she acknowledged her, Riley grinned.

With the weight of the trucker's stare pressed tight against her back, she focused on the task at hand. She made breakfast, divided scrambled eggs onto plates, cutting toast into bite size pieces. She'd used the last of both. She'd have to stop at the store on her way to work. Lucky for her, her boss let her keep groceries in the walk-in during her shift. Rationing milk into sippy cups, she stole a glance out the kitchen window. Her mother's beat-up, old Camero was gone. It wasn't even 8AM. Kelly never opened her eyes before noon, let alone got dressed and—

"You're fuckin' that Indian kid."

The voice behind her had gravel in it, rough and pitted from too many cigarettes. Her hands jerked, sloshing milk over the side of the cup while she tightened the lid. She hadn't even heard him move. Someone that big shouldn't be allowed to move so quietly.

He was close; she could smell the warm beer on his breath. Feel it against her neck. He leaned into her, planting a large, heavy hand on the scarred Formica counter, hemming her in. She took a sliding step in the opposite direction, not daring to turn until she was clear of him.

"What," he drawled, turning to lean against the counter, beefy arms crossed over his barrel chest. "You don't know how to talk unless you got a coffee pot in your hand?"

She'd been friendly to him the night before. Smiled and chatted while she re-filled his coffee. Brought him his food. Handed him a container of pie and apologized for closing early. What kind of pie had she given him? Remembering Jed's outburst, what he'd said, stained her cheeks with shame.

She set Jason's cup on his tray and turned. "I don't know what you're talking about," she said, forcing as much conviction as she could find into her tone to combat the cold spike of fear that shafted through her.

He knew about her and Tommy. Suddenly, looking into the flat, mud-brown eyes of the man in front of her, Tommy's insistence that they keep their relationship a secret didn't seem so ridiculous.

The nasty grin that worked its way across the trucker's face told her he knew he'd scared her. That he'd meant to. That he liked it. "Yeah, you do." He tilted his head to give her a smile that looked more like a sneer. "No swingin' dick comes charging to the rescue like that without good reason," he said, the laugh that followed sounding like a shovel hitting a pile of hot asphalt—black and sticky. "He's been at you, good and proper... I'm just wondering if he knows you're givin' it up to that Carson kid too."

"That's a lie." The words ripped out of her, their claws leaving holes in her chest, making it hard to breathe.

You taste like peaches.

It'd happened last month at school. Daydreaming, as she often did in chem class, she'd doodled through the bell, not noticing the room was rapidly emptying. The final bell jerked her in her seat and she began shoving books and papers into her bag, giving a startled yelp when she heard her name being whispered in her ear. "You waitin' on me, Melissa?"

Jed. She shot to her feet and turned, running into the solid wall of his chest and her hands went up, instinctively attempting to fend him off. "No, I just—"

He leaned into her, pinning her against one of the heavy lab table, making escape impossible. "You aren't afraid of me are you?" He brought a hand up, laying it on her collarbone, the heel of it pressed against the place where her heart was trying to bounce out of her chest.

She couldn't speak, her tongue thick and useless, glued to the roof of her mouth. She shook her head and he laughed at her, taking her fear for something else.

"Just relax," he said to her, lids heavy over warm hazel eyes. "If you don't like, I'll stop… promise."

He kissed her and she let him—going still as she allowed the firm pressure of Jed's lips on hers. He must've taken her lack of resistance as encouragement because the slant of his mouth suddenly intensified, went heavy with the kind of desperation that turned her fear to something close to terror.

He groaned, shoving his tongue into her mouth with so much force tears sprang instantly to her eyes. The hand at her hip clamped tight, holding her in place while he pushed himself into the space between her thighs, grinding his erection against her.

Breaking away, she turned her face to the side. "Jed, please…" she whispered, her eyes wheeling toward the closed classroom door. This was the last period of the day. School was over. No one was coming. No one knew she was in here. Not that anyone would care. She was Kelly Walker's daughter. That made anything that happened here—anything he did to her—her fault. "Please stop."

Instead of stepping back, her plea moved him closer.

He buried his face in her exposed neck, inhaling deeply against her skin. "Remember the first time I kissed you," he whispered, his words hot against her jaw, the hand between them dipping lower to cup her breast, squeezing her so hard, tears sprang to her eyes. "Remember what I said?"

Panic, quick and razor sharp, struck deep. Stealing the air from her lungs. Anchoring her feet to the floor. She did remember. She remembered being sprawled in the dirt where he'd shoved her after she'd rejected him. It'd been her eleventh birthday. "You're gonna be my girl, Melissa—*mine*," he'd hissed at her, his fists clenched at his sides, handsome face contorted with anger.

Five years later, Jed still hadn't given up. If anything, he'd become more determined. She planted her hands on his chest; prepared to push him as hard as she could when, just like that day in the woods, his attention was drawn away from her.

A janitor opened the door, pulling his cart behind him, stalling in the doorway, blinking stupidly at the scene he'd walked in on. Jed's hands instantly dropped, his hips shifting away from hers so that she could breathe again. He looked down at her, leaning into her again, just for a moment. "You taste like peaches," he whispered in her ear before walking away as if nothing had happened.

Now, a month later she could still hear him, feel the way his words wormed their way into her ear. He thought what'd happened had been consensual and why wouldn't he? She'd let him kiss her. Had stood there and cried like a scared little girl while he put his hands on her. Anger curled in her belly, wrapped tight around the lump of shame that had been lodged there since it happened.

Behind her, Riley let out a whimper, recalling her attention and she turned to see the little girl staring up at her, blue eyes filled with tears, food going cold on the tray in front of her.

"It's okay, Ri," she said, softening her voice. "Eat your breakfast. Everything's okay." The lie came out so smooth, for a moment she almost believed it.

"Yeah, kid—everything's just *peachy...*" the trucker said, letting his words trail off for a moment. "Maybe she wants her milk." Reaching behind his back, he produced a pink sippy cup and waggled it at her, daring her to take it.

Very much aware that the twins were watching her, she moved away from the table, forcing herself across the worn linoleum that covered the warped floorboards of the trailer. Stopping a few feet in front of him, Melissa reached out and took the cup from his outstretched hand, her eyes never wavering from his. Once free of the cup, Pete's hand shot toward her wrist and snaked around it with lightning speed, pulling her close. He breathed beer fumes in her face as he stared down at her, leering over her.

She froze, just like she had with Jed—the fear that iced her gut bringing on a wave of self-disgust. "Let go of me," she said, her tone low and even, making promises she knew she could never keep.

The trucker laughed at her. "Or what? You gonna run tell your daddy?" He shook his head, the look he gave her making her feel naked despite the loose T-shirt and flannel pants she wore. "I got news for you, little girl— your daddy already knows you're a whore. No need to run off and tell him," he said, his fingers tightening painfully around her wrist.

She looked away, her eyes instantly finding the wooden baseball bat she kept propped against the wall behind the front door. She'd used it a few time to run off some of her mother's dates who'd gotten a bit too rough or decided that sex with Kelly wasn't worth the money they paid. Most of them had been locals—more afraid of the fact that her father was the chief of police than a teenage girl with a bat.

"How 'bout that other one ? The kid with the high n' tight, drinking coffee and reading in the back." He shook a finger at her, head cocked, eyes mean. "You fuckin' him too?"

Michael. He was talking about Michael. Her throat went dry. All she could do was shake her head in denial while she jerked helplessly against the hold he had on her.

"We're gonna have fun, you and me." He grinned at her, revealing teeth stained the color of weak tea. "Just you wait and see…" Laughter bubbled on his lips but he let her go. She stepped back, removing herself from his reach.

She opened her mouth, unsure of what was going to come out but then the front door banged open. Kelly teetered in on a pair of scuffed high heels, her legs banded to mid-thigh by an impossibly tight denim miniskirt. One hand gripped a paper wrapped bottle of what Melissa would bet a week's worth of tips was the cheapest brand of vodka she could find while the others had its fingers threaded through the plastic webbing of a six-pack. The moment she saw her, her mother's eyes narrowed suspiciously while she bounced a look between the two of them.

"What's goin' on?" she said, the cigarette dangling from her lips bobbing with each word. Behind her Riley had stopped crying. Jason had gone quiet too—both of them staring at the woman who was technically their mother. She scared them with her screeching voice and drunken stumble. She hadn't touched them—*not once*— since she'd given birth to them. Melissa thought she might kill her if she tried.

"Nothing," she said, turning away from the way the trucker ran a possessive hand over Kelly's backside as she walked past him, his eyes never leaving her face.

Kelly set the paper-wrapped bottle and the bundle of cans on the counter, taking a drag before scissoring the cigarette from her mouth to blow out a stream of smoke. "Don't look like nothin'." She aimed a look at the trucker. "She's an uppity little bitch," she said, pressing her breasts against his arm as she leaned over him to retrieve a plastic tumbler from the cabinet he stood in front of. "Gets it from my mother." She cooed it in his ear, shooting her a glare over his shoulder.

The trucker's arm snaked around Kelly's waist, fingers digging into her hip as he pulled her closer. "No worries, baby," he said, shooting her another look. "We were just getting to know each other, is all."

Kelly's expression soured a bit but she managed a smile. "Don't bother," she said never taking her eyes off the trucker. "Girl wouldn't know how to have fun if it ran up and bit her in the ass," She thrust the cup in her direction with a smirk. "Make me a drink."

It was something Kelly made her do whenever she could. Her mother's way of making her feel small and powerless because she knew how much she hated doing it. She could feel the trucker watching her. Waiting for her to show herself. To either stand up to her mother or do as she'd been told.

She hesitated a moment too long and the cup rocketed through the air, bouncing off Jason's tray before hitting the floor in a noisy clatter. His eyes widened for a second before his face crumpled, his features dissolving in a squall of tears. They were a year and a half old. Too young to understand what was happening around them. Too small to be so scared all the time. From her seat next to her brother, Riley stared at Kelly with a look of wary caution that would ripen into hatred before too long.

She turned her back on the pair of them. A dangerous thing but she did it anyway to smooth a shaking hand over Jason's cheek where the cup had struck him before hitting the floor. Her fingers brushed at the red welt the cup had left while she made cooing sounds, trying to quiet him. "It's okay. You're okay, I'm right here. You're—"

"Shut that fuckin' brat up and fix me my goddamned drink." Kelly's tone left no doubt that there would be consequences if she didn't comply.

Hunkering down, Melissa reached for the cup while Jason squalled and Riley sat in the kind of detached silence that scared her more than the crying. She didn't realize until she tried to pick the cup up off the floor that the hand she had stretched out in front of her was clenched in a fist.

She forced her fingers to relax enough to pick up the cup and stood, carrying it to the refrigerator. There, she filled it with ice before making her way over to the counter, Jason's sobs tapering off into a roundabout of watery hiccups behind her.

Melissa pulled the bottle of rot-gut from its brown paper sleeve and cracked the cap, twisting it off as fast as she could. The trucker was watching her over Kelly's shoulder—his hooded gaze on her face, an intrusion she could barely stomach.

Tipping the bottle over the cup, she poured nearly the entire contents over ice, the vodka's fumes stinging her eyes. She recapped the bottle to preserve what little was left and pushed it back along the counter until it hit the wall. If one of the twins got ahold of it and spilled it, there'd be hell to pay.

She pressed the drink into Kelly's waiting hand. "I gotta go," she said as she moved. "Double shift at the diner."

"Don't leave them here," Kelly called after her, the ice in her cup rattling as she lifted it to take a drink. "Pete and me have plans, ain't that right, Daddy?"

"That's right, baby," the trucker all but growled, taking the tumbler out of Kelly's hand before he started to maul her.

Melissa's stomach heaved. Sometimes the fact that they shared DNA was too much to consider. It was easier to pretend they were strangers. That this woman she lived with was not her mother. She took the twins out of their highchairs, hefting Jason onto her hip before offering her hand to Riley. Riley preferred to walk.

On her way to her room, she risked a last look into the kitchen. Pete had Kelly's skirt rucked up around her hips, his blunt, heavy fingers buried in the white flesh of her bare ass. His mouth was open, tongue thrusting in and out of her mother's gaping mouth—a crude preview of what was to come. She looked away, hurrying down the hall as fast as towing two toddlers would allow.

It wasn't what they were doing that made her sick. It was the fact that when she'd looked back, while her mother was on her knees working the front of his pants open, Pete had been staring straight at her.

FIVE

MELISSA DRESSED THE TWINS and set them in the playpen she kept in her room before pulling a clean uniform out of her closet. She tossed it onto her bed before locking her bedroom door. Pete hovered somewhere under six-foot but he was thick. His bull neck and beefy arms promised that if he was so inclined, a hollow-core door and cheap privacy lock would offer no protection.

She could hear them. The grunts and moans had started not long after she'd shut her door and from the sounds of it, they were still in the kitchen. Kelly had made it sound like Pete would be sticking around... she looked at her door again and thought about the way he'd watched her while she poured her mother's drink. Stared at her while her mother had her face between his legs.

She was going to need a better lock.

She changed clothes in a hurry, buttoning the front of the faded yellow uniform before tying on her starched white apron. Dale, the owner of the diner and Tommy's uncle, was old-school. He liked his waitresses clean, pressed and punctual. The first two she could handle. With a pair of toddlers to care for and a mother who was fall-down drunk most of the time, the punctual part was tough.

She looked at the cheap alarm clock on the TV tray that served as a nightstand. She had less than an hour to get the twins to the sitter and still make it to work on time. From the sounds coming at her from down the hall, what was going on in the kitchen wasn't going to stop any time soon.

Ducking back into her closet, Melissa stooped down to reach into a hole the size of her fist that had been kicked into the wall by some previous tenant. Inside it was a zippered pouch stuffed with cash. Nearly three hundred dollars.

Every cent she'd managed to scrape together over the past month that wasn't spent on rent and utilities. WIC and food stamps took care of the majority of their grocery needs but government assistance required her mother's participation. Getting her to the welfare office in Marshall was sometimes more trouble than it was worth. Sometimes she had to ask her grandmother for help.

It was something she hated doing. Even though her grandmother claimed she understood, she'd been heartbroken when she'd decided to moved back to Jessup to live with Kelly. She'd done it for Jason and Riley, knowing that neither of them would survive without someone sober to take care of them. Her grandmother knew that but her leaving still hurt her.

She unzipped the pouch and pulled out a few random bills, stuffing them into the pocket of last night's stained apron. She knew Kelly searched her room. Stole money when she could. She also knew she was lazy. If she found a few bucks in an apron pocket, she'd stop looking. Even as erratic and impulsive as she was, Kelly was predictable.

Operating on instinct, she stuffed the pouch into the twins' diaper bag before hefting it onto her shoulder. Pete's presence changed everything. She could no longer trust her mother to be predictable.

Sliding open her bedroom window, she dropped the diaper bag onto the ground before turning to lift the twins from their playpen. She climbed out the window, dropping the few feet to the ground. Jason's face appeared at the window and she lifted him through, followed by Riley.

Settling her brother on her hip and taking her sister by the hand, she led them into the trees directly behind their trailer.

Their trailer park was surrounded by a thick stand of trees on three sides, a fourth tree line running down its middle. The left side of the park was for people who owned their homes. Lower-middle class who worked hard and took pride in what was theirs. The right side served as a sort of housing project for Jessup's welfare population. That's where she lived.

Taking slow, careful steps, Melissa led Riley through the trees and bramble, weaving this way and that to avoid low slung branches. Readjusting Jason on her hip, she let out a small sigh when Riley pulled her tiny hand from hers and began to toddle ahead. "Careful, Ri—stay here with me," she called out even though she already knew that the little girl would do as she pleased.

Riley was about ten steps ahead of her when she saw it.

"*Stop*," she called out, her voice firm enough to stall the toddler in her tracks. The wooded area that surrounded and divided the trailer park was a popular default hangout spot.

When no one's parents were gone for the weekend, the town kids—the ones from good families who lived in the big houses that lined the well-kept streets just north of the town square—who usually denied ever stepping foot in this trailer park would hang out in the trees, drinking and smoking the dope they scored from the dimly-lit trailers that lined the right side of the court. Sometimes their partying got out of hand. Sometimes they got carried away. Sometimes they'd throw loose change at her window and laugh about how she was a whore, just like her mother.

They'd keep her awake at night with their raised voices and vicious taunts. But last night had been quiet. What had Wade said? That they were all hanging out at Rob Duffy's house. His parents had gone to New Orleans for the week.

It'd been quiet. No one had been in the woods behind her house last night. The pair of underwear lying on the ground in front of her said different. She pulled Riley away and set Jason down beside her.

"Stay here for me, okay?" she said to them and they stood close together, watching her while she crouched down, pulling the diaper bag off her shoulder. Rooting around inside it, she came up with one of the plastic grocery bags she used to wrap up dirty diapers. Fitting it over her hand she picked up the underwear, ready to wad them up and tie the bag closed so she could throw them away. But then she looked at them.

They were hers. Her white cotton underwear. The ones with the scratchy lace around the legs and the pink satin rosette in the front. She looked close. There was something crusty and stiff stuck between the fold...

She jerked her face away from the bag the moment she realized what it was, shame splotched against her neck. She looked around, confused—expecting to see a bunch of town kids giggling behind a tree at the joke they'd made of her. There was no one there. Just Jason and Riley standing a few feet away, watching her in that way they had. They knew something was wrong and had decided to be very still and quiet until it was safe to move again.

She'd worn them Wednesday. She remembered because the lace trim around the legs had driven her crazy all shift. She'd worn them and then thrown them in the dirty clothes basket in her closet, vowing to cut the lace off of them before she wore them again. She looked up, aiming her face toward the back of her trailer. Her bedroom window was directly in front of her, no more than thirty feet away.

Getting her underwear would be an easy thing. Anyone with a few bucks in his pocket was welcome into Kelly's bed. She was at the diner most nights. It would take only a few minutes to duck into her room afterward and take what you wanted. Someone had stolen her underwear and then stood here and watched her while they—

She swallowed the lump of disgusted embarrassment that threatened to choke her. For some reason, Jed Carson's face swam in front of her.

Tying the bag off, she jammed it into the pocket of her apron before gathering the twins and hurrying through the trees to the other side of the trailer park.

What could she do with them? Take them to her father? She could imagine dropping them on his desk, explaining what they were. Where they'd come from.

She could just hear it—him telling her that all a pair of her semen-covered underwear in the woods behind her house proved was that she was a whore, just like her mother.

Telling Tommy would cause a different kind of trouble entirely. He'd automatically assume it was Jed—just as she had—and do something stupid. Something that would get him arrested or worse.

She couldn't tell her father. She couldn't tell Tommy. She couldn't tell anyone.

As usual, she was on her own.

SIX

SHE'D TOLD KELLY SHE had a double shift at the diner but that was a lie.

She'd get off at three o'clock and if she was lucky, make it across town in time to make the 3:10 bus to Marshall. She tried to get there at least once a month to see her grandmother and to deposit money into the savings account Lucy had started for her when she was a little girl. She'd managed to save over five thousand dollars in the year and a half she'd worked at the diner. Her escape plan if things really got bad. The sudden appearance of Pete and what she'd found in the woods behind the trailer this morning told her that it was no longer a question of *if* things got bad but a promise of *when*.

After she'd dropped the twins off at Mrs. Kirkland's, she'd thrown the underwear in the dumpster near the entrance to the trailer park. There was no way she could tell someone without making herself look bad. No one would believe her. Not even Tommy.

It was best to forget about it. Move on. One of her mother's customers had found her underwear and used them to masturbate while he watched her undress. Disgusting and mortifying but there was nothing she could do about it without causing more trouble for herself.

She walked through the back door of the diner and into to the kitchen, expecting see Tommy working the grill but he was nowhere to be seen. Instead, Dale— Tommy's uncle and the diner's owner—stood at the flat top, flipping burgers. As soon as she walked in, he cut a look at the clock above the ticket window. She'd made it without a second to spare.

"You sure cut it close, don't ya?" Dale said with no real heat, shifting over to drop a basket of fries into the fryer.

She thought about what she'd been doing a half hour ago. Examining a pair of defiled underwear left outside her window. Realizing they were hers. Throwing them away because there was no one she could tell who would believe her. "Sorry. Jason's got a cold. He was fussing all night," she said, hanging her purse on the hook next to the door. If she wasn't careful, lying was going to become a habit. "Where's Tommy?" she said, hoping the question sounded casual.

Dale shrugged. "Called late last night, told me he was gonna jump a bus and head up to see his mom for the day. Last minute but it saves me having to pay him a days' wage," he said, reaching over to lift the fries from the fryer, giving them a shake before dumping them into the bin. "He also told me what happened last night. Said he closed early so he could walk you home."

Panic seized her chest. She needed this job. Couldn't support Jason and Riley without it. If Dale fired her... "I'm really sorry," she said, the words tumbling out of her mouth in rush. "I know I promised you that hiring me wouldn't cause you any problems but—"

Dale held up a hand. "Quit your yammerin', girl. You ain't done nothing to cause me trouble." He shook a generous amount of salt onto the hot, greasy fries. "Truth is, I told Tommy anytime he thought you needed it, that he was to close up and get you home safe."

She stared at him for a moment, unsure of what to say. Tears pricked the corner of her eyes and she swallowed hard in order to clear her throat of the emotion that suddenly gathered there. "Thank you, Dale," she said, opening her mouth to say more. She could tell him. About Pete. About what she'd found in the woods. Why she'd really been late. He'd believe her. He'd help her. "I—"

"No gettin' weepy on me, girl," he said, grabbing a few buns from the bin, splitting them before popping them onto the grill. He shot a look at her purse. "You want to put that in my office?" He knew that she kept a bank account in Marshall. He also knew that this was the first Saturday in weeks that she wasn't scheduled to work a double shift.

She thought about the wad of cash she had stuffed in it and nodded. "Thanks, Dale," she said, sliding it off the hook.

He grunted, jerking his chin at her. "Hurry it up— we're busy and Terri can't go five minutes without complainin' about her feet."

She nodded and hurried into his office to drop her purse in the bottom drawer of his desk. Tommy had gone to see his mother. She lived in Oklahoma somewhere. Tallulah Onewolf called herself a free spirit. Folks in Jessup called her a crazy hippy. So crazy that she'd actually named her half-Apache son, Tomahawk. He'd talked about taking her to meet his mother someday but now...

She pushed the thought aside. Whatever was going on between Tommy and her, whatever happened, there was little she could do about it now.

"Terri's got the counter today. Only way I can keep her bitchin' to a minimum," Dale called after her as she moved through the kitchen. She usually worked the counter and the bank of booths that lined the front of the restaurant while Terri worked the back tables and booths but she didn't complain. Jed and Wade sat in one of her usual booths, along with Shelley and some other kids from school. The last thing she needed was to deal with that mess.

"Okay," she said, shooting Dale a smile over her shoulder on her way through the swinging door that connected the dining room to the kitchen. The second she stepped into the dining room, Jed turned his attention on her like he knew she was there. Like he'd been waiting for her.

Dale was right—this was the busiest Saturday they'd had in a while and she was grateful for it. Within seconds, she was lost in the diner's hectic rhythm. Delivering food and cleaning up spills. Taking orders and re-filling coffee cups.

Michael O'Shea was in a booth next to the waitress station—the same place he'd been sitting the night before. He glanced her way before lifting his cup to his mouth to take a drink. He had a book in his other hand and had obviously been there for a while but she didn't remember taking his drink order or filling his cup.

"How long have you been here?" she said, tipping more coffee into his nearly empty cup and he shrugged.

"A while." He slipped a scrap of paper between the pages of the book in his hand and set it aside to add sugar and cream to his cup. "I got here about the same time you did," he said, twirling his spoon a few times. He took a testing sip before setting it down.

"I don't remember seating you," she said stupidly.

"You didn't. You looked busy so I sat myself," he said, looking up at her innocently. "Got my own coffee too." He cocked his head at the waitress station. "Terri's cool with it. Keeps me out of her hair."

There was something about his tone, the way he looked at her. He didn't scare her the way Jed did. Or give her butterflies like Tommy. When Michael O'Shea looked at her, she felt exposed. Challenged. Like he saw things in her he wasn't supposed to. That no one else did. For some reason, it made her angry.

"Does Terri also let you loiter?" she bit out, her tone harsher than she intended.

He smirked at her. "Define *loiter*," he said before raising his cup.

Her fingers tightened around the coffee pot in her hand. "We're really busy today. If you're not going to order anything besides coffee, I'm gonna have to ask you—"

Something flickered in his eyes, deepening his gaze from gray to something a few shades darker. "I could go for some pie," he said before picking up his book.

It wasn't the words that threw her. It was the way he looked at her when he said them. Like he knew what they meant. Her spine went stiff and from some reason her thoughts bounced back to what she found in the woods.

He shifted his gaze back to the pages of his book. "Pecan. A la Mode. Please," he said to the page he was reading.

She stood there for a few seconds, unsure of what just happened or how to react. Michael turned the page in his book.

She finally moved. Back to the lunch counter where she ignored the hole Jed was staring into the top of her head while she cut Michael's pie. His girlfriend sat next to him, clinging to his arm. As long as Shelley was around, he'd keep his distance.

"He's back," Terri said in a sing-song voice beside her, clipping her own ticket to the wheel. "And he ain't too happy havin' this old bird taking his order."

"I imagine not," she said, transferring the piece of pie to a plate before sticking it in the microwave. "But he won't kick up too much fuss with Shelley here."

Terri laughed, scooping ice into a plastic pitcher. "You heard from Tommy?"

The microwave dinged and she took the pie out, careful to seem uninterested in the other waitress's question. "Not since last night." She added the ice cream before picking up the plate. "Do you usually let Michael O'Shea serve himself?"

"You bet your sweet ass I do," Terri says, filling the pitcher with iced tea. "The kid comes in and seats himself. He's quiet, gets his own coffee and leaves me a twenty for an eighty-five cent cup of coffee."

Before she could answer, the bell above the door chimed, signaling a new customer. She looked up to see Chief Bauer walk in with his deputy, Zeke.

This day just kept getting better.

Picking up the plate she carried it, weaving her way between tables, toward the back of the diner. "Anything else," she said, plunking the pie onto the table in front of Michael who barely glanced at her. From the corner of her eye she could see her father and Zeke, take a seat in her station.

"Nope," he said, attention focused on the book in his hand.

She shifted from foot to foot, trying to see his face past the book in his hand. *Using Map and Compass* by Don Geary. "Is that a good book?" she said, stalling. Not wanting to turn around and face her father. Not today.

"Good?" Michael laughed and turned the page without looking at her. "That's not a word I'd use to describe it."

From the corner of her eye, she could see her father, just feet away from where she stood. He was listening to her conversation. "Then why are you reading it?"

"Because its required." He slipped his piece of paper into the book again and set it aside. Finding his fork, he dug it into the pie's gooey center.

What had he told Tommy yesterday? He'd been accepted into Ranger school. "For the Army?"

Instead of answering her, he looked up at her. "Thought you were busy," Michael said, smiling up at her around a mouthful of pie.

She jerked back, stung. "I am." Ripping his ticket off her pad, she slid it across the table. "Pay up front when you're finished."

He sighed, lowering his fork. "Shit. Wait—"

She turned. Her father usually sat in Terri's station. Probably to avoid her but today doing so had planted him directly in her path. He and Zeke sat at a table across from Michael's booth. Zeke looked uncomfortable. Her father looked like he'd swallowed a bug. Getting up and switching sections was out of the question. It would just draw more attention and speculation than usual. He was stuck. They both were.

Snagging a fresh pot of coffee from the station, she made her way over. "Chief Bauer. Deputy Ramsey," she said, filling their cups. "What can I get you?" *Besides a new waitress.*

"Hey, Melissa," Zeke said before shooting his boss a nervous smile. "Who's at the grill today?"

"Dale's on today—Tommy had to go see his mom," she said, setting the coffee pot to the side so she could retrieve her order pad.

Her father huffed out a disgusted snort. "Poor excuse for a mama if you ask me," he said under his breath, face buried in a menu even though he probably had it memorized.

"I didn't," she said, snapping her father's attention to her face. "Matter of fact, I don't remember asking you a damn thing." She held his gaze, counting to five. She'd never spoken directly to him before—not ever. He was her father. Everyone knew it. Talked about it. Even now she could feel the whole diner poised, waiting to see how things would play out between them. She looked away from him and found Michael watching her from across the aisle. For some reason, seeing him made it possible for her breathe again.

"You want the usual, Zeke?" she said, shifting her attention to the deputy. He was a regular at her counter when her father wasn't around and he was always kind to her.

Today was no exception. "Yes, ma'am," he said, handing her his menu.

She took the menu, tucking it under her arm before turning her smile on her father. "What can I get you, Chief?" she said, pen poised above her pad.

"Meatloaf. Extra gravy on the potatoes." He held the menu out to her, letting his gaze stray past her to rest on Michael, lip curling in undisguised disgust before he let his gaze wander back to her face, his expression saying it all. He'd seen her trying to strike up a conversation with Michael and thought she was flirting. That she was trash, just like her mother. She was surprised by how much it hurt, how quick he was to believe the worst in her.

She yanked the menu out of his hand, mouth open to tell him to go to hell. Before she could speak, Michael leaned into the aisle, his quiet gaze aimed straight at her father.

"Not to worry, Chief—*your daughter* wouldn't piss on me if I were on fire." He said it loud. Loud enough so that his voice traveled around the diner, killing conversations and drawing stares. "Matter of fact—" He slid out of the booth and stood, reaching into his pocket to pull out his wallet. "The only reason she hasn't tossed the entire contents of that coffee pot in her hand into my face is the fact that she was raised by one of the sweetest, kindest people I know." He flipped a bill onto the table before tucking his wallet away while giving her father the same asshole smirk he'd just given her. "And I think we both know I'm not talking about her mother. Or you."

Michael picked up his book and strolled through the dining room, past a few dozen patrons on his way out the door. All of them watching him go, whispering about him and what he'd just done and the girl he'd done it for.

SEVEN

THE REST OF HER SHIFT flew by. Chief Bauer fell back into his habit of ignoring her while he ate, the closest thing he came to speaking to her was a disgruntled nod when she offered to re-fill his coffee cup. Zeke over compensated by making useless conversation and tipping her twice as much as usual. "Sorry," he muttered at her, stuffing a wad of bills into her hand before hurrying after his boss.

As soon as he left, Melissa cleared Michael's booth and wiped down the table. A one hundred dollar bill stared up at her from where he'd tossed it. Who left that kind of tip for a cup of coffee and a piece of pie? Remembering what Terri said, she decided he'd accidently left her a hundred instead of a twenty in his hurry to get away from her. As much as she needed it, she decided she couldn't keep it and she quickly pocketed the money. She'd give it back the next time she saw him.

Three o'clock found her in the supply closet, doing the weekly inventory for Dale; clipboard in hand as she counted cans of ketchup. After the lunch rush the diner cleared out, leaving nothing more than a few road dusty truckers at the counter with Terri and her with nothing to do.

"You better get goin' if you're gonna make your bus," Dale said, poking his head through the door. He had her purse in his hand.

Shit. A quick glance at her watch had her dropping the clipboard on the shelf next to a row of gallon-sized jars of mayo and grabbing for her sweater. "Thanks, Dale," she said, hurrying as she pulled it on. It was only a few minutes after three but the chances of her making the bus to Marshall were slim. Still, she took her purse from his grip and smiled. "See you tomorrow morning," she said as she hurried out the back door, slinging her purse over her shoulder.

"I need you here at 7 AM," Dale called after her, moving back toward the grill he'd been cleaning. "6:59 would be better."

"Okay," she shouted behind her, flying past the dumpster and into the parking lot. She didn't get more than a few steps when she spotted the bus to Marshall in the distance, pulling away from the terminal curb, earlier than usual. She stopped running, her shoulders slumped forward. There wouldn't be another bus until tomorrow morning. She was stuck.

"So… you and Onewolf, huh?"

The voice caught her off guard but what it said scared her, reminding her of Pete. She whipped toward it, hands clutched in a death grip around the strap of her purse. "Excuse me?"

Michael sat on the trunk of a car she recognized as having once belonging to his father. It was an old muscle car, lovingly restored. Painted a gun metal gray that sparkled in the afternoon sun. The color of it matched his eyes perfectly. He looked up from the book in his lap, shooting her a smirk. "You. Tommy. Two little love birds and all that shit."

"Are you following me?" She thought about the pair of panties she found in the woods that morning. *Her* panties. Dried stiff, cover in... she took a step toward him without even realizing it. "Are you? Was it you outside my window last night?"

His face changed, the smirk that rode his mouth falling into a frown, his gaze darkening to the color of soot. "What?"

Something about his face, the stillness of it, scared her as she took a step back, away from him. "Never mind," she mumbled as she dug into the pocket of her apron. "Here, I think you left this by mistake." She pressed the money he'd left her into his hand before turning to leave him to whatever it was he was doing. She caught movement from the corner of her eye a split second before she felt his hand clamp roughly around her bicep, stopping her retreat. She looked, first at where his hand connected with her and then at his face—too scared to move.

"Are you in trouble?" he said to her, his hand still firmly gripped around her arm. She thought about everything that had happened to her in the last twenty-four hours. Her fight with Tommy. Her mother's latest boyfriend making advances toward her. The underwear she found in the woods outside her bedroom window. Stolen from her room. Defiled and discarded.

Yes. For just a moment, she was certain that she could tell him. That he would help her. Believe her. And then she remembered who he was. The things he'd done. The trouble and pain he'd caused his parents. "No." She yanked her arm out of his grip. "And even if I was," she said, following up her denial. "What would you do about it? Make promises to help me and then abandon me like you did your little sister?"

The look he gave her told her that mentioning Frankie was a mistake. His face had been still—passive—before but now... now there was nothing passive about the way he was looking at her. She took another step back but he didn't move. Didn't lash out at her like she expected him to.

"We can't all be saints, Melissa." He smirked at her again, sliding off the trunk of the car he was sitting on to stand over her while she fought the urge to take another step back. "Some of us can barely keep from drowning in the shit we're swimmin' in."

She opened her mouth to answer, shame instantly staining her cheeks. "I'm—"

"Hey!"

Relieved, she turned toward the voice to see Wade standing in the parking lot, a few yards away. "Hey, Wade," she said, finally able to take that step back she'd been fighting. "What are you doing here?"

"Jed and Shelley decided on a movie after lunch and three's a crowd. I was just drivin' by and I saw..." Wade's gaze strayed over her shoulder, finding Michael's. "You need a ride home?" he finished, a slight frown creasing his usually smooth brow.

"She's not going home," Michael said behind her. "She's going to Marshall and she missed her bus. I was just about to offer her a ride."

She turned to find him looking down at her, his face passive again. Eyes quiet. How had he known she'd been on her way to Marshall? What was he doing here, sitting in the parking lot nearly three hours after he'd left the diner? Had he been waiting for her? If so, what for?

Before she could ask, Wade spoke up. "I'll take you, Melissa. Wherever you want to go," he said behind her, sounding both confused and concerned to find her in the diner parking lot, talking to Michael O'Shea, of all people.

"I'm not a bad guy." Michael said to her. Something lurked behind his words. Something that said he didn't even believe himself when he said them.

"Yes you are," she whispered. "You're parents loved you and you hurt them. Your sister needed you and you abandoned her. Stay away from me."

She turned away from him, halfway expecting him to grab her arm again but he didn't. He left her go—but she could feel his watchful eyes on her as she crossed the parking lot, toward Wade.

"Are you sure you want to take me all the way to Marshall?" she said, stopping in front of him, suddenly uncomfortable with the situation. Wade was her brother. Something they'd never actually acknowledged between them. Being alone in a car with him for an hour would more than likely lend itself to awkward conversation. But she needed to get to Marshall. "I mean, I can pay you. Give you gas money—" she reached into her apron, fingers closing around the zippered pouch she kept her tips in.

"Keep your money," he said quickly, hand up to fend her off. "I mean, what else have I got to do on a Saturday afternoon?" Wade smiled at her as he pulled the passenger door open for her and she got in, anxious to get away from the way Michael was looking at her.

He cast a glance over his shoulder at Michael as he slammed it shut. "See you around, O'Shea," he said, offering the other young man a wave as he rounded the back of the car and got in to start the engine.

As they pulled out of the parking lot, Melissa took a glance in the rearview mirror. Michael stood where she'd left him, watching them drive away—his expression as unreadable as ever.

EIGHT

"LET'S JUST GET IT out of the way—whaddya say?"

They'd been driving in awkward silence for nearly thirty minutes and it was killing her. Melissa looked up from her lap, where her hands kept twisting and untwisting themselves in her apron. "Get what out of the way?" she said, even though she was sure she knew exactly what he was talking about.

Wade cut her a quick glance, his expression bland as he rolled his eyes. "Come on, Melissa—it's just you and me here." He winced a bit, suddenly looking as uncomfortable as she felt. "Your mom. My dad... *our* dad," he said, leveling his gaze on the road again. "We've never really talked about it, is all. Don't you think we should?"

We've never really talked, period. "What's there to talk about?" She shrugged, forcing her fingers to stop their incessant twisting. "My mom's a whore and your dad had the misfortune of knocking her up on while he was home from college for Christmas break." She marveled at how unaffected she sounded. How hardened she'd become against the facts that shaped her life. Billy Bauer had been nineteen—Jessup's golden boy. Kelly, only fifteen but already so beautiful it was almost painful to look at her, had been nothing but a walking, talking pile of trouble. No one knew what kind of promises had been made. What kind of plans. How they really felt about each other.

All they knew was that they'd been involved for a short time before Billy had gone off to college and for a while, off and on, afterward. When Kelly turned up pregnant, everyone naturally assumed that he was the father and a paternity test had confirmed it. Rather than come home and marry her, Billy came home already married—wife and newborn son in tow.

With his wavy, light brown hair and clear, hazel eyes set over a firm, square jaw, Wade looked like a younger version of their father. Sometimes, it made looking at him hard. Now was one of those times. She shrugged again to ward off the sudden and unwelcome sting of tears. "You're my brother. Talking about it isn't going to make it any more or less true."

"So you admit it." Wade shot her a sheepish grin. "As such, I'd like to invoke my brotherly rights and ask you a question."

He looked so relieved, so happy that she felt her own trepidation fade and she found herself grinning back. "Okay."

"What's going on between you and Michael O'Shea?"

The grin on her face changed shape, feeling more like a grimace. "Nothing," she said, looking away again.

"I gotta tell you... what I saw this afternoon didn't look like nothing," he said, rubbing the back of his neck, obviously uncomfortable again. "It looked like a whole lotta *somethin'*."

"Then you were looking at it wrong," she said, hoping her tone was firm enough to close the subject. No such luck.

"Look, I'm just sayin—he's bad news. Dad—*Billy*—has had him in holding at the station so many times he practically lived there. Drunk and disorderly. Assault. Trespassing. Robbery... you know he ran away awhile back, before his parents died." He stopped talking for a moment, waiting for her to nod before continuing. "They found him in Dallas, ODed on heroin in a closet in some rent-by-the-hour motel. Same room his real mother died in." Wade shook his head. "Michael O'Shea is screwed beyond recognition, Melissa. A nice girl like you wouldn't last five minutes with a guy like that."

She found herself wanting to defend Michael, to explain things someone like Wade couldn't possibly know. What living like that was like. What it did to you. Who it made you into.

We can't all be saints, Melissa... some of us can barely keep from drowning in the shit we're swimmin' in.

Remembering what Michael said to her instantly shamed her but instead of defending him, she asked the obvious. "How do you know all that?" She knew that

Michael got into trouble often, that he'd been a constant source of pain and embarrassment for the couple who adopted him but she'd never heard the details until now.

Wade cocked another shoulder at her, shooting her another sheepish grin to go with it. "I work at the station sometimes—filing and taking calls. I might have looked at his record."

For some reason, the admission made her angry but she kept it to herself. "Well, you don't have to worry. I barely know Michael O'Shea and I plan on keeping it that way." She looked out the window, the WELCOME TO MASHALL sign a red and white blur as they blew past it. "Besides, I don't have time for that kind of stuff."

"What kind of stuff?"

"Boys. I'm too busy working and taking care of Jason and Riley," she said, slightly panicked at the hard knot of bitterness she heard in her own voice.

"... So then, those rumors about you and Tommy are completely unfounded?"

His question tugged at her, demanded an immediate denial but, despite the fact that the small knot of panic exploded into full blown fear, she simply shot him a puzzled look and did her best to remain calm.

"Tommy? Tommy Onewolf?" She turned toward the window so he couldn't see her face. "Not even," she said, forcing as much disgust into her voice as possible.

First Jed, then both Pete and Michael and now Wade. That meant people were talking. Speculating. About her and Tommy. Just like that had about her mother and Billy. How long before the rumors reached her father's ears? Last night she'd been sure she didn't care if he knew but now…

"Is this about what Jed said last night?," she said, careful to keep her tone even. "He was totally wasted. You know how he gets when he's been drinking."

"It's not the drinking that makes him act that way." Wade muttered it, just loud enough for her to hear and it stained her cheeks red.

"I never asked for that… for him to follow me everywhere." She looked at him. "I wish he'd just go on and marry Shelley already and leave me alone."

"Yeah, like marrying her would help…" Wade's voice trailed off. "You know Shelley's just a substitute, right?"

"A substitute?" she said as the car slowed, the sparely populated roadside becoming clogged with buildings and cars. Marshall was ten times the size of Jessup. It had chain stores and two high schools. Melissa had never traveled any further than here. For her, this is where the world ended. "A substitute for what?"

"For you." Wade shook his head, exiting off the highway and onto Marshall's main street. "He loves you," he said, suddenly sounding uncomfortable again. "Has since we were kids. Sometimes, I think maybe too much." He made a left onto Pinecrest before taking an immediate right into the bank parking lot. "Look, Michael. Tommy—none of it's any of my business but Jed doesn't see it that way."

Melissa's memory suddenly flashed on that day in the woods outside the church. Her eleventh birthday—the day Jed had pushed her down for rejecting him. He'd been standing over, fist clenched. Glaring down at her with more pent up anger and frustration than she'd even seen before.

You're gonna be my girl, Melissa. Mine...

She felt strange. Hot and cold all at once. Like someone had yanked her in from a blizzard and thrust her into a raging fire. It made her dizzy.

Wade was still talking, pleading his friend's case. "He loves you—he just doesn't know how to show it without acting like a total asshole." He pulled the car into a slot outside the bank and put it in park before turning to look at her. "He'd never hurt you. I'd bet my life on it," he said, sounding so sure, for a moment, she almost believed him. "But Tommy Onewolf is another matter altogether." He was warning her. Pushing the boundaries of his friendship with Jed as far as he dared. Funny, he wasn't lodging any veiled threats at Michael O'Shea. For some reason, the thought of Jed attacking Michael didn't worry her. Not even a little bit.

Melissa tugged on the door handle, popping it open so she could stick her leg out. She didn't want to talk about Jed anymore. "I'm not the girl for Jed," she said, softening her rejections of his best friend with a smile. "I'm not the girl for anyone. That includes Tommy." She opened the door wider and slid through it so she was standing beside the car. "Thanks for the ride," she said, bending at the waist to look at Wade.

"You want me to wait? I can—" He sounded like he didn't want to leave her. Like he wanted to protect her, but she just shook her head.

"No, I'm going to go see my grandma for a bit—she'll give me a ride home," she said, straightening before shutting the car door. "Thanks again…"

"Anytime." He smiled like he meant it, shifting his car into reverse and backing out of the parking lot and driving away.

<u>NINE</u>

"WILL THERE BE ANYTHING else, Ms. Walker?"

Melissa looked at the deposit slip in her hand. Even with keeping out an extra forty dollars, she had almost six thousand saved up. Seeing the sum printed out always made her feel calm. Like she had a plan. A way out. This time, she didn't feel calm. She felt a sense of inevitability. The sum was no longer a comfort, it was a fortune told. A prophecy, on the cusp of being realized.

She was going to leave Jessup. Soon.

It scared her, knowing that. That she was going to leave behind everything and everyone she knew—well, almost everyone. When she left, Jason and Riley would be going with her.

"No. Thanks, Jenny." She looked at the bank teller and smiled. "See you in a few weeks."

She left the bank, walking across the strip mall parking lot. There was a mom and pop hardware store facing the main road—she'd spotted it when Wade pulled into the bank.

Finding the aisle with the door locks was easy, but that's as far as she got. Realizing that installing a new lock on her bedroom door would take more know-how than she possessed, she faltered.

"Help you find something?" The old man behind the counter said to her, scooting around it to shuffle in her direction. He was wearing thick red suspenders and house slippers, a patch with the name *George* sewn onto the breast pocket of his shirt.

"I need a new lock..." she looked at him and smiled, hoping it made her seem less helpless. "Probably more than one."

"For privacy or security?" he said, digging his hands into his pants, jiggling his keys while he sized her up.

She thought about the ridiculous, push button lock she had now. "Security. My neighborhood isn't the greatest and—"

George nodded his head and *harrumphed* at her. "You're Lucy's girl, ain't ya?"

"I'm her granddaughter," she corrected, not wanting this man to mistake her for her mother.

"Know your way around a drill?"

She shook her head. She didn't even own a screwdriver.

He nodded, pulled his hands out of his pockets. "This is the one you want then." He reached past her to lift a heavy-looking security chain off the rack. "Come on," he said, shuffling back to the counter. "Let's get you sorted."

SHE walked the few blocks to her grandmother's house quickly, her shiny new lock buried in the bottom of her purse. She'd told Wade that her grandmother would drive her home but she said it without being entirely sure that she'd be able to. For a moment she regretted her impulsivity. The bus back to Jessup wouldn't leave until nine PM. She'd promised Mrs. Kirkland that she'd be back to get the twins no later than seven o'clock. If her grandma couldn't take her home then she didn't know what she'd do.

Relief washed over her when she turned up the driveway. Parked under the shaded carport of her grandma's rental was her 1989 LeBaron. She was home.

"Grandma," she called out, letting herself in through the back door, into a tidy kitchen that smelled of lemons and strong coffee. She took a deep breath, holding it in her lungs. She missed it. Living here. Being safe.

"I'm in here," her grandma answered back. "Cut yourself a piece of cake and I'll be right in." Melissa smiled; picturing her tiny frame hunched over the basket of mending that supplemented the death benefits she received from her grandfather. She remembered sitting with her, patching holes and stitching seams as a little girl, weaving her needle through fabric with a surprisingly steady hand. She missed it. The simplicity of her life here. It'd been only two years since she'd left but if felt like a lifetime ago.

She'd been fourteen when she'd made the decision to move in with her mother. Kelly showed up on her Grandma's doorstep and even though she'd never seen her before, not in even in a picture, Melissa knew who she was because Kelly was undoubtedly the most beautiful woman she had ever seen.

Her hair, a deep rich auburn floated down her back in lazy waves and curls, lying against soft pale skin that was just beginning to dull. Her eyes, the color of the sky on a cloudless summer day, were a little murky but in the right light, still looked clear and bright. Her features were still stunning as it was difficult to disrupt bone structure.

It was like looking in a mirror.

"Well, hey there, girl! Come give your mama a squeeze!" Kelly squealed when she walked through the back door. As soon as she heard the words, Melissa felt a hot knot of dread form in her belly. Grandma Lu was sitting at the kitchen table across from Kelly, smoke curling in the air from the cigarette that dangled from her mother's mouth. She took a long drag before blowing out a stream of smoke in her direction.

"Well, ain'tcha gonna say nothin'?" Kelly said, her pretty mouth poking out in a gesture Melissa was sure usually got her whatever she wanted. Lucy looked scared but she gave a slight nod, silently urging her to speak to her mother.

It was first time Melissa could remember wanting to defy her.

"What's the matter; she didn't teach you no manners?" Pouting hadn't worked so an edge crept into Kelly's voice, hard and sharp. "She been tell you lies about me?"

Melissa set her backpack on the counter and turned toward the woman that called herself her mother and opened her mouth, not sure what was going to come out, praying that whatever it was, wouldn't embarrass her grandmother. "No, I'm surprised to see you is all." She felt lame; introducing herself to her own mother, as she put out her hand to be shook. "We've never met, I'm Melissa."

Kelly let out a high-pitched peel of laughter as she crushed out the cigarette in her hand, using the cake plate in front of her rather than the ashtray her grandmother had undoubtedly provided. "Well, ain't you proper? I bet this one *just* loves you," Kelly said, jerking her head toward Lucy as she stood, a sour expression on her lovely face. Melissa felt her breath catch in her throat, strangling her. Her mother was obviously pregnant; her rounded belly jutting out from her perfectly shaped hips.

Melissa's eyes flew to her grandmother's face and she felt a lump form in the back of her throat. Lucy sat quietly, her hands folded on the table in front of her as she returned her gaze. Looking at her, one word formed in Melissa's mind and threatened to bring tears to her eyes.

Grace.

Throughout this entire ordeal, not just the fourteen years that Melissa had been alive but the nearly thirty years she'd been the mother of Kelly Jean Walker, her grandmother had managed to keep her grace. How was a mystery to Melissa but knowing that she had filled her with pride and in that moment, Melissa was awestruck by her grandmother's strength.

The hand that hung in the air between them was ignored as Kelly threw her arms around her and squeezed her tight, the swollen mound of her belly making it awkward. As she felt the hard press of flesh between them, Melissa suddenly realized what she was feeling. Her sibling, a brother or sister, trapped in that body.

Defenseless. Alone.

It was the exact moment she realized that when Kelly left, she'd be leaving with her.

SHE could hear Lucy moving down the hall, pulling her away from the memory. "Well, now," her grandma said as she came through the doorway. "I wasn't expecting to see you today." Lucy smiled, patting her cheek as she passed the table where she sat, on her way to the coffee pot.

"I had some stuff to do," she said, forking a bite of lemon pound cake into her mouth to discourage questions. "Are you busy today?"

Lucy chuckled, carrying her cup to the table to sit down across from her. "Mrs. Steiger gained back forty of those fifty pounds she lost on that crash diet she was on. I've got a pile of slacks and four Sunday dresses that needs to be let out; along with a moth-eaten wool coat she swears she can't live without, though I've never seen her wear it." The amusement in her grandmother's eyes faded away as soon as she sat down, her gaze finally resting on her face. "What happened?" she said, her tone no longer light.

She picked up her fork again and used it to mash moist, yellow crumbs into the plate in front of her. "Nothing... specific. Kelly was particularly horrible this morning is all," she said, giving her a shrug. It felt wrong, complaining about her mother to Lucy. She'd made the choice to move in with her, against her grandma's wishes. To whine about it now was ridiculous.

"Girl—you are a terrible liar." Lucy lifted her cup and took a drink, waiting for her to tell her the truth. When she didn't, she set the cup back down, reaching out a hand to wrap it around her wrist to stop her from mashing the entire slice of cake as flat as a piece of paper. "You tell me what's going on—right now, Melissa Jean."

She looked up from the plate in front of her, intending to lie. Her grandmother was right—she was terrible at it but what could Lucy do? Instead she dropped the fork, twisting her hand inside the old lady's grasp to hold onto her. She told her everything, starting with the scene Jed had made at the diner the night before and ending with the painfully awkward car ride with Wade.

Lucy listened quietly, carefully to keep her face composed. She'd always been like that. Like a sponge— absorbing messes and spills without complaint. When she ran out of words, Lucy patted her wrist and sat back in her chair, pulling herself from her grip. Before she even opened her mouth, Melissa knew what she would tell her to do.

"I can't, grandma." She pushed her chair back and stood, walking her half-eaten plate of cake to the trashcan. "I *won't*, so don't even say it," she said, scraping her fork against the plate. The cake peeled off in one bright, yellow clump. Her grandmother wanted her to go to her father for help.

"Okay, Miss *I-Can-Handle-It*, do you have a better idea?" Lucy folded careful fingers on top of the table and glared at her. "Because, from where I'm sitting, helping you is his *job* on multiple levels."

She was quiet for a few moments, probably one or two too long because her grandmother hissed out a pain-filled breath. "Melissa Jean don't you even *think* it."

"I can't stay there anymore," she said, setting her plate gently into the bottom of the sink. "It's not safe." She turned quickly, quicker than Lucy had expected her to. She caught the tremble of her mouth an instant before she pressed it into a grim line. "For them or for me."

"Then you'll come here," Lucy said in that matter-of-fact way she had. The one that told her there was no use in arguing. "You'll bring Jason and Riley here and I'll petition the court for custody. I'll get a lawyer—"

She thought of the trucker at table six—Pete. The way he'd watched her. Looked at her while he touched her mother. Running away to her elderly grandmother's wouldn't stop him. But she couldn't say that. She couldn't tell Lucy that she wasn't strong enough to protect her.

"You can't afford a lawyer, Grandma," she said instead, trying her best to be gentle. "Neither of us can."

"You'll come here," Lucy repeated stubbornly, pushing her own chair away from the table to stand, facing her down. "You'll come home—where you belong."

Melissa sighed and nodded her head. "Okay, Grandma," she said. "Okay."

Every time she told a lie, it got easier. She sounded so convincing, so relaxed that for a moment, even she believed the words rolling off her tongue.

Pretty soon, she'd be a professional.

TEN

SHE WAS QUIET ON the way home, listening to her grandmother make plans. Nodding her head and smiling at the appropriate times while she made plans of her own.

Tomorrow was Sunday and the bank was closed. When she'd started depositing money into the account, she'd declined a debit card, not wanting her mother to find it. Now, she regretted it. It meant she'd have to wait until the bank opened on Monday morning before she had access to her money.

The car rocked gently on its axils as they pulled close to the curb in front of Mrs. Kirkland's tidy trailer house and she got out to collect the twins. It was after seven which meant she was late but Mrs. Kirkland didn't seem to mind—the extra twenty Melissa slipped into her hand along with her weekly payment didn't hurt.

Putting the diaper bag in the back and Riley on the seat between them, Melissa held Jason on her lap on the short ride home. She'd have to think about buying a car once they got where they were going which meant car seats for two. So many expenses she never really considered… instead of worrying about it, she buried her face in Jason soft coppery hair and took a deep breath. He smelled clean, like Mrs. Kirkland had given him a bath. A new babysitter—just one more things she'd have to find once she left this place.

"That man your mother's got her claws in—Pete." Lucy said, taking the long way through the park, giving herself a few extra minutes. "He got a bad tattoo of a spider on the back of his hand?"

Melissa could see it, muddled and thick, the cheap ink of it bled into the skin of his hand when he grabbed her. "Yes." She nodded.

"That's Pete Conners. He grew up here—went to school with your mama. I heard he was back but I'd hoped it was nothing more than a nasty rumor." Lucy pulled into the shallow dirt drive next to their trailer and put the car into park. "I'll wait while you pack," Lucy said, her jaw set a stubborn angle.

Melissa smiled. "Grandma, I have to work a double tomorrow," she said, thankful that this time she was able to tell her grandmother the truth. "Monday, okay? That'll give me time to pack up and give Dale notice. I'll call you Monday."

Lucy looked skeptical for a moment, like she was going to argue with her. Like she knew she was lying but then she looked past her and something like relief passed over her face. Melissa looked over her shoulder in the same direction as her grandmother. Behind her, Michael O'Shea was sitting on her plywood and cinderblock porch like he'd been waiting for her to come home.

"Hello, Michael, how's your sister?" Lucy said like they were old friends. Like it wasn't at all odd that he would be sitting in the dark outside her granddaughter's house.

Michael offered Lucy the kind of smile Melissa had never seen him wear before—open and genuine. "She's really good, Mrs. Walker. I wish she'd stop growing so fast," he said, shifting his gaze from Lucy's face to hers for just a moment. "Need some help?"

It was an echo of the question he'd asked her earlier only this time he seemed to know she couldn't refuse him without upsetting her grandmother. Still… "No, I can—"

"Nonsense," her grandmother said, her tone shutting down her rebuttal before it even really began. Lucy leaned across the seat, answering him through the open passenger window. "If you could grab the diaper bag, you'd be a world of help." She smiled her approval when Michael stood to do as she asked.

"I don't need his— "

"*Manners*," Lucy hissed at her under her breath as he pulled the rear door open behind her and shouldered the bag on the back seat. Then he opened her door and stood back for her to exit. For a split instant she considered slamming it closed so she could open it herself. Instead she leaned over and dropped a kiss on her grandmother's soft cheek. "I love you," she said before she started to scoot across the seat. Lucy caught her by her wrist, anchoring her inside the car.

"If something happens…" she looked past her, over her shoulder, at the dilapidated trailer. "You'll call him."

For a moment, Melissa thought she meant Michael but then she understood. Lucy was talking about her father again. She sighed. "Grandma—"

"Promise me." Lucy tightened her grip on her wrist. "You promise me right now, Melissa Jean or I'm gonna go in there and—"

"Okay," she looked her grandmother in the eye and nodded. "Okay. I promise."

Lucy smiled and let her go, watching her slide across the bench seat to stand in the dirt next to Michael, Jason riding her hip. Without asking he bent down, the bag slung over his back and held his hand out to Riley.

"She won't let you carry her. She likes to walk on her—"

Riley took Michael's hand and let him pull her into his arms, as easy breathing. He hefted her onto his hip and she laid a sleepy head on his shoulder. He shot her a smirk over Riley's head.

Asshole. Fighting the urge to say it out loud, she gave her grandmother a final wave and mounted the shaky steps. Michael and Riley followed behind.

She opened the front door, holding it for Michael to pass through before shutting it. Smoke drift toward her from the living room where a burning cigarette glowed in the dark. The tip of it brightened for a moment, following another stream of smoke blown in their direction. It was too dark for her to see who it was but she knew it was Pete. He was waiting for her. Despite herself, she was glad Michael was with her.

Leaving Pete behind, she stepped left, entering the kitchen area. The trash can was lying on its side in the middle of the room, empty beer cans and fast food wrappers strew across the floor. Half-eaten food and trash cluttered the counters. Dirty dishes piled high in the sink. It looked as if someone had trashed it on purpose.

"Sorry," she muttered as she shuffled her way through the mess, her cheeks stinging with embarrassment. "It was clean when I left this morning."

"Don't apologize," Michael said following behind her. His voice sounded strange. Tight, like he could barely move his jaw to form the words. She didn't have to look at him to know he was angry.

She led him down the hall to her room. The twins usually slept in the small room next to hers but not tonight. Not with Pete around. She watched while he laid Riley in the playpen beside her brother. She looked around her room with its saggy mattress and stained carpet. The dingy walls and threadbare sheet that served as a curtain over her window. Nothing like the nice, clean home he grew up in.

The sting of embarrassment deepened into near mortification but he didn't seem to notice. After laying Riley down, he waited for her to do the same with Jason. When it was done, they stood there for a few moments, drowning in awkward silence. Aside from Tommy, she'd never allowed another boy into her room before.

"I need help," blurted out. Before she could think better of it, she dug into her purse and pulled out the security chain she'd bought earlier. "The man at the hardware store said it'd be easy to install on my own but I don't even have..."

Michael looked past her, gazed fixed and steady on the wall behind her like he could see through it. Like he could see Pete sitting in the living room and knew he was the reason she'd bought the lock. He reached into the back pocket of his jeans and pulled out what looked like a large pocket knife.

"Let me see it," he said, gesturing for the lock and she handed it over. The pocket knife turned out to be a multi-tool. Michael opened the Phillips-head and had her new lock installed in less than fifteen minutes.

"Here," he said, handing it to her. "I've got another one." He offered her a small smile before he exited, leaving her alone.

She shut her door, set the multi-tool on her nightstand. Sliding the new chain in place, she stepped out of her waitressing uniform, exchanging it for a baggy T-shirt and a pair of worn flannel pants with faded yellow stars on them.

Jason and Riley were already asleep so she clicked off the bedside lamp and shut the door behind her. Back in the kitchen, she found Michael leaning against the kitchen counter, staring into the darkened pit of her living room, hands dug into the pockets of his jeans.

"What are you doing here?" she said, trying to distract him. Without thinking, she started to clean the mess that'd been made while she was gone.

"It's my birthday."

She stopped cleaning. Looked away from him and listened. Music—80's glam rock—floated toward her from down the hall. Under the music she could hear it. Grunts and moans. The rhythmic banging of her mother's headboard against the thin trailer wall. If she stood still enough, if she closed her eyes, she could almost feel the trailer sway around her with the force of it.

Her mother was open for business.

"Oh," she said, dumping the armful of beer cans she held against her chest into the trash can. "Happy birthday."

"An old buddy of mine thought I'd want to..." he shook his head, unable to meet her gaze. "That's not why I'm here though."

"It's none of my business," she said, tossing an empty vodka bottle into the garbage hard enough to shatter it. The sound of it breaking was oddly satisfying. "Why should you be any different from the other five hundred men who live in this town?"

"I've *never*—" He rubbed a hand across his mouth, muttering something to himself before shaking his head. "Look—I came here to make sure you're okay before I leave, that's all," he said. "Are you? Okay?"

Behind him, the tip of Pete's cigarette glowed cherry-red in the dark. Smoke drifted through the gloom. He was watching. Listening. Waiting for Michael to leave.

"I'm fine," she waved a hand around the kitchen before throwing a half-eaten fast food hamburger in the direction of the garbage can. "Can't you tell?"

He laughed but he didn't sound amused. He sounded like he understood. Hearing it reminded her of what Wade had told her about him. About the drug overdose and how his birth mother had died. How he'd lived before Sophia and Sean O'Shea had opened their home to him. Made him a part of their family.

"You're leaving?" she said, expecting to feel relief. She didn't. What she felt was angry. "Didn't you just get here?"

"Yeah, but… coming home was a mistake." He was having a hard time looking at her again. "It's not my home anymore. Stopped being my home when they died."

They. He was talking about his parents.

"So that's it?" Her tone hardened, her voice gaining volume. "A few days of taking Frankie to the park and out for ice cream and you're done?"

Instead of yelling back, he nodded. "It's best for her that way."

"Bullshit. It's just best for *you*." She said, throwing another bottle in the trash. The curse jerked his gaze toward hers. He seemed surprised she'd even think the word, much less say it out loud. "You're leaving for the same reason you left before—because you're too selfish and lazy to stay."

"Really?" he said, sounding irritated all of a sudden. "We're having this conversation again?"

"You think I like it here? You think I don't have options? That I'm stuck here?" The sound of another smashed bottle punctuated her words. "I stay for *them*— and if you were a halfway decent human being, you'd stay for Frankie." She had no idea why she was saying it—any of it. Hadn't he been decent to her? Hadn't he just helped her? None of that mattered. Right now, all that mattered was that he was leaving his sister behind and that made him a coward.

All he did was pull his hands out of his pockets but like before, in the parking lot of the diner, she fought the urge to flinch away from him. "But I'm not, am I?" he said, his lip curled up at her in a vicious sneer. "I'm not a decent human being—not even halfway." His anger sucked the air out of the room, creating a vacuum that made it hard to breathe. "I'm a sack-of-shit loser who fucks up everything he touches, right? *Right?*"

Before she could answer him, her mother's bedroom door opened down the hall. A few seconds later, Allen Wickem, one of Michael's old drug buddies, strolled into the room, zipping up his fly. "I knew you'd change your mind," he said, when he saw Michael standing there, shooting him a grin through the mess of lank brown hair that crowded around his face. He smelled like her mother. Cheap vodka, even cheaper sex and marijuana.

"She's all warmed up and waiting…" he stalled out; his gaze shifting to follow Michael's which was still aimed at her. The grin on his face morphed into a leer. He gathered his greasy hair and tied it back with the rubber band he kept around his wrist, revealing pock-marked cheeks that were hollowed out by too many drugs and not enough sleep.

"Hey, Melissa," Allen slurred, digging his hand into the front pocket of his dirty jeans. "I still got some money left if you wanna take a ride on my—" The loose change in his hand pinged and rolled across the kitchen floor as he was grabbed by his throat and given a rough shake. A nickel bounced off the leg of her pants and bowled along the floor before it dropped into one of the floor vents. She didn't watch it roll. All she could do was stand perfectly still and stare, confused by what was happening in front of her.

"Apologize," Michael growled, giving Allen another shake, hard enough that she was sure she heard his neck crack.

"What the fuck," Allen gurgled, stunned as he clawed at the sudden grip around his neck. "I was just jokin'—"

"Am I laughing?" Blunt, steady fingers constricted, digging in tight enough to cut off Allen's air supply. "Am I *fucking* laughing?" Michael whispered in his ear.

"No… no, Mikey," he said, his Adam's apple scraping against the vise-like grip Michael had on his throat. "You ain't laughin'."

"Apologize." He said it again, his eyes never leaving hers.

"I'm sorry—I'm sorry, Meliss…" Allen croaked, his eyes wheeling around to find her, bulging in there sockets. "Mikey, I can't breathe—I can't—"

"If you ever come back here—if you even so much as *look* at her again," Michael whispered in his friend's ear, his tone dead calm, his eyes as flat and black as stones. "I'll find you and break your goddamned neck." Before Allen could stutter out a response, Michael spun around, tossing his friend in the direction of the front door.

Allen stumbled into it, knocking over the Louisville Slugger she kept propped in the corner. "I'm sorry, I'm sorry…" He scrambled to pick it up, putting it back in its place. "I'm sorry," he said a final time, throwing her a look over his shoulder, eager for her approval, before scrambling out the door.

For a moment they just stood there, neither of them moving.

"What was that?" she breathed quietly. Her hands rattled against her thighs, hanging from shock-slackened arms. "Why did you do that?"

"*Shit…*" The word came out, more sigh than curse. He shook his head, hand rubbing the back of his neck, jaw set at a dangerous angle. "I'm sorry. I just—"

She aimed her gaze at the floor. It was scattered with change and beer caps. Fast food wrappers and empty bottles. Things people discarded that no longer served a purpose. She thought about the nickel that'd rolled into the floor vent. It would rattle now, every time she turned on the heat. Remind her of what had just happened and how it got there.

"You're still the same." She looked up at him now. "No matter how different you think you are—you're still the same."

The look on his face said he agreed with her and he nodded, like she was right to be afraid of him but when he opened his mouth, all he said was, "See you around." He followed his friend out the door without so much as a backward glance.

As soon as the door slammed shut behind him, Melissa moved. Unsure of where to go or what do, she stooped over to pick up a wadded up burger wrapper by her foot. Behind her, a sound reached out from the dark living room, the flick of a lighter followed by a plume of cigarette smoke.

"Sure you ain't fuckin' him?"

Pete. He'd seen the whole thing. Heard it all. Cheeks burning with shame, she dropped the wad of paper into the trashcan and turned toward the hall. Another sound followed her, pushing her to move faster and faster.

Laughter. Brutal and rough. Pete was laughing at her. Telling her exactly what he thought of her.

She closed her bedroom door on the sound, thumbing the privacy latch before sliding the security chain across the jam. Fifteen minutes ago, seeing it made her feel safe. Now it made her feel stupid. A couple of locks weren't going to keep Pete out. Nothing would.

Suddenly, Monday seemed a lifetime away.

ELEVEN

SHE DIDN'T SLEEP. Spent all night staring at the clock and listening to Pete move around the trailer. Up and down the hallway. Stop outside her bedroom door. Give the cheap doorknob and push lock a jiggle. Over and over until it suddenly popped open and the door too, banging against the security chain she'd slid into place before she'd gone to bed.

"When I'm ready, there ain't nothin' that'll keep me from it," he said, laughing at her, face pressed into the wedge, the short length of chain holding the door closed strung against his cheek. "You ain't stoppin' me and neither will these shitty locks."

She didn't answer him. Didn't want to antagonize him. She just lay there, waiting for him to kick the door in. To get it over with. He didn't. He just stared at her for a few moments before he walked away, laughing.

So, she didn't sleep. Didn't move. Just stared at the gap his absence had created, willing time to move forward. As soon as the clock said 5:30 AM she got up. Pete had been quiet for a few hours. Probably passed out in the living room or in her mother's bed. Either way, she didn't want to risk it. Dressing as quietly as possible, she woke the twins, remembering to slip the chain off the door before she left out the window, to carry them through the woods to Mrs. Kirkland's.

She made it to the diner by 6:45. Dale was there to offer her a grunt of approval before he disappeared into his office, leaving her and Tommy alone. She watched him for a few seconds while he scraped the grill and switched on the fryers.

"Morning," he said to her over his shoulder like nothing was wrong. Like he hadn't disappeared yesterday without so much as a word to her. Like they hadn't been fighting the night before that.

"Good morning," she answered back, her tone stiff and polite. "How's your mom?" she added and the question gave him pause. He stopped scraping and looked at her.

"She's good," he said over his shoulder. "Getting ready to leave for some kind of artist residency in New Mexico." He cracked a couple of eggs onto the grill. "You want bacon in it?" he called through the pass-through. Confused, Melissa shouldered her way through the door while she tied her apron.

They opened at 7 AM on Sundays and there was usually a line of people at the door waiting to get in for breakfast before they hurried off to the nine o'clock church service. The fact that Michael O'Shea was sitting at the otherwise deserted lunch counter should have surprised her—but it didn't.

"Come on—that's not a real question, is it?" Michael answered back while he watched her over the rim of his coffee cup. He sounded like himself. Not the boy who'd installed her lock or defended her against his scumbag friend. He sounded like the *old* him. The Michael who drank too much and ended up in handcuffs. This Michael she knew. This Michael she knew how to deal with.

Tommy laughed while she stared back at Michael, trying to figure out what he was doing. Why he was here. He seemed to know it because he chuckled in her direction while he set his cup back in its saucer. "Don't hurt yourself, sweetheart," he said to her. "I just stopped in for a breakfast burrito before I hit the road."

An ugly, red flush stung her cheeks. To combat it, she pulled a to-go cup from the stack under the counter and filled it with strong, black coffee. She set the cup in front of him along with a plastic lid, and a pile of sugar packets and creamer cups. "For the road," she said, her tone pointed and sharp.

He laughed at her again.

Just then, Tommy pushed through the swinging door, two large, foil-wrapped burritos in his hand. "Dale says they're on the house," he said, sliding them into a white paper bag and setting it on the counter next to the coffee. "He lost a son in Desert Storm."

Michael stood, offering them both a grim smile. "I remember... tell him I said thanks," he said, rolling down the top of the bag before fitting the lid she'd tossed on the counter onto the to-go cup. He took both and moved toward the door while Tommy headed for the kitchen.

It was seven o'clock so she followed him to the door to open it up for day. Through the Mylared glass, Melissa could see a tight cluster of people waiting to get in. She reached for the deadbolt and twisted the lock to open the door. "Thanks for the coffee," he said to her, leaning against the glass to push the door open with his shoulder.

"You're welcome," she said after him, feeling stiff and awkward as she watched him move across the parking lot for a few moments. Regulars filed in and she got to work, heading toward the counter where several people were already seated.

Lifting Michael's cup from the spot he'd been sitting, she started to wipe the counter but stopped short. Under the saucer was a hundred dollar bill—the same bill she'd returned to him yesterday—something scrawled in heavy black marker across its face.

It wasn't a mistake.

TERRY called in sick, so her breakfast/lunch shift stretched out until well after dark. It was just her on the floor and Tommy at the grill with Dale bussing tables. When she was finally able to flip the *closed* sign over and lock the door, her feet were throbbing. Including the money Michael had left for her, she had over four hundred dollars in tips stuffed into her apron pocket.

"Go on home, girl," Dale told her, taking the cloth she was using to wipe down the counter out of her hand and slinging it over his shoulder. "I'll take care of the rest—get some sleep."

It was as close to a *thank you* as she'd ever gotten from Dale and she took it with a nod and grateful smile. "Thanks, Dale," she said. "See tomorrow after school."

"Go ahead and take it off—Terry'll be here, even if I have to drag her in by her hair." He was rubbing down ketchup bottles while he spoke. "Still need you for the day after though—Tuesday's Bible study."

Every Tuesday, the Baptist church's women bible study group came in for lunch and gossip after they spent the morning extolling each other's virtues. None of them liked her. She nodded, pushing a flat smile across her face. "I'll be here."

She lifted her purse from the hook and slung it onto her shoulder, moving slow—trying to give Tommy a chance to offer to walk her home. He didn't. He just scraped away at the grill in front of him like his life depended on it. She left without saying goodbye.

Forty-five minutes later, she mounted the rickety porch steps with two toddlers in tow—Jason dozing, cheek pressed against her shoulder while she pulled a half-asleep Riley up the steps after her. Even exhausted, she insisted on walking on her own.

Inside it was dark and quiet. Sundays were slow for Kelly—family men tended to stay with their families.

Lust-bitten high schoolers had school in the morning. Thinking of school and the homework she still hadn't gotten around to, she shuffled in and closed the door as quietly as she could. Things seemed calm. She wanted to keep them that way. Homework could wait. Now she just wanted to rest.

Tucking the twins into the playpen in her room, she made quick work of gathering her tips—or most of them anyway. Leaving several random bills in her apron pocket, she stuffed the rest into the hole in her closet wall before she made her way back to the kitchen. She was tempting fate, she knew—but she was hungry. The last thing she'd eaten was half a club sandwich at lunchtime, stealing a bite here and there between tables. It was after ten o'clock now.

Opening the fridge, she remembered that she still hadn't gone to the grocery store. All the stale-smelling space had to offer her was a gallon of milk with about a half-inch left in the bottom, a grubby-looking bottle of mustard and a few pieces of bologna that had started to turn brown around the edges. She left the milk for Jason and Riley, praying that it'd still be there in the morning. Grabbing the rest of it, she set it on the counter.

She found a few pieces of stale bread in the cabinet— the heels. Her mother hated the heels. She wasn't a fan either but right now, she didn't care. Squirting mustard onto the face of the bread, she built her sad sandwich in the dark, adding the bologna and more mustard to drown out its taste. If its smell was any indication, eating it was a gamble. She didn't care about that either. Closing it up, the kitchen light snapped on, just as she lifted it off the counter to take a bite.

"Where you been?"

She lowered the sandwich and turned to find her mother standing in the middle of the kitchen, glaring at her. "At work," she said. "Terry called in so I had to stay until close." She watched as her mother yanked the refrigerator door open, aiming a disgusted look inside.

"Not one stitch of food in this house," Kelly grumbled, swiping the near empty milk jug off the shelf. Lifting it to her mouth, she drained it, eyes locked on her the entire time. Her mother hated milk almost as much as she hated the heels of the bread. It wasn't that she wanted it. It was that she didn't want anyone else to have it. Not even her own children.

Kelly tossed the empty jug in the direction of the garbage can and missed. Droplets of milk splotched against the wall, adding themselves to the collection of near misses. "This place is filthy," she said, itching for a fight. Kelly was a mean drunk. She was even meaner when she was dry.

Right now she was stone sober.

She thought of the twins, asleep in the next room. Little arms and fingers clutching at each other. Faces pinched with worry, even while they slept. Instead of fighting she tried to appease. "Dale gave me the afternoon off, mama. I'll stay home from school tomorrow," she said in a moment of inspiration. "I'll clean, go to the store. It'll be done by the time you wake up—promise."

Kelly glared at her, blue eyes narrowed by hatred and something else. Something that shamed her. Made it hard to keep looking at her. "Tomorrow morning don't feed me tonight, does it?"

Her mother wasn't hungry. Her mother wanted a fight and she wasn't going to let up until she got one. Melissa held out the sandwich, offering it to Kelly, knowing what her mother would do before it even happened. Kelly's hand lashed out, smacking the sandwich from her grip. It fell apart before it hit the floor, gravity pulling old bologna and stale bread, mustard-side down, onto the grimy floor with an audible *splat*, yellow ooze peeking out around their edges.

"I want real food—not this shit you keep buying." Kelly's eyes dropped to the front of her apron—to the pocket where she'd stuffed her tips. She held her hand out without saying a word.

Giving without a protest wouldn't do. Her mother was mean but she wasn't stupid. If she just handed it over, she'd get suspicious. Start wondering where the rest of it was. "Mama, it's Sunday night. Everything is—"

The hand that'd slapped the sandwich lashed out, cracking across her face with enough stink to pop her eardrum and bring on the rush of tears.

"Gimme," Kelly said, wiggling her fingers in a *give it here* gesture she knew well. Melissa hesitated for a few seconds, long enough to have her mother rearing back again, before she dug into her apron pocket.

"Here," she said, shoving the money at her mother's hand. "Take it." A little over a hundred dollars. It was money well spent if it meant her mother would leave.

Kelly grabbed at the wad of cash, fast and sure. She didn't drop a single bill. Looking down at it, she scoffed. "That's it? You worked all day and this is all you made?" She said it like her daughter was a sucker for even trying.

"I had to pay Mrs. Kirkland," she said, fast on her feet. She paid the sitter every Saturday but her mother didn't know that.

"That old bitch..." Kelly muttered, tightening her grip on the fistful of money. She glared at her for a few more seconds before she dropped her gaze to the ruined sandwich on the floor.

"Clean up your mess," Kelly said before she walked out the front door.

TWELVE

SHE DID AS SHE WAS told, wiping up congealed mustard and old bread with a few napkins she found stuffed in a random drawer, dropping the lot of it into the trash can. Her stomach still growling, she ate a handful of dry cereal before heading back down the hall. Her hands were stained yellow. They smelled like mustard.

Alone, she decided to chance a shower. Stripping down, Melissa hung her uniform on the back of the door and jumped in to scrub herself before the water even had time to warm. Ten minutes later she was clean, drying herself off with the last clean towel she could find. Dale giving her the day off was a Godsend.

Down the hall, the front door banged open just as she was shutting her own for the night. Her mother, back from wherever she'd gone and it sounded like she wasn't alone. She could hear her mother giggling, a low, male voice speaking in hushed, urgent tones. Probably a long-haul trucker who'd spent one too many lonely nights on the road, willing to pay a few bucks for Kelly's company.

Whoever it was, it wasn't Pete. As relieved as she was, she knew he wouldn't stay gone for long. He'd be back.

She shut the door with a quiet click, pushing in the lock and sliding the chain across the door jamb even though both had been proven useless. She thought of the bat she kept propped next to the front door. Right now, it did her no good. Then she remembered the multi-tool Michael had given her. As quietly as she could, she reached out, finding it on the TV tray next to her bed. Wrapping her fingers around it, she pulled it to her, tucking it under her pillow.

Lying down, she pressed her back against the wall, gaze, fixed and unblinking, on the door knob—waiting for it to turn...

SHE must've dozed off because the next thing she heard were footsteps outside her window, a second before someone tapped on the cracked glass of it. She lay there, frozen by fear, listening. Beyond her door, the trailer was its own version of quiet. Loud music, muffled by a closed bedroom door. Beneath the music, the sounds of sex, bought and paid for.

The tapping again. This time a bit louder. More insistent. She got up, reaching for the bed sheet that covered the window, moving it so she could see outside, the multi-tool Michael gave her clenched in her fist.

Tommy stood on the other side of the glass, hands dug into the pockets of his MU hoodie. As soon as she moved the sheet, he took a step away from the window to look up at her.

Relief bled into her hands and they trembled as she unlatched the window and slid it open along its track. She crossed her arms over her chest, peering past him, into the dark. The thick line of trees behind him seemed heavy. Like it was hiding something. Something waiting, just outside her field of vision. "What are you doing here, Tommy?"

Tommy grinned but the shine of it didn't reach the dark of his eyes. He was remembering their last conversation. Their fight. The question she'd asked him that he hadn't been able to answer.

Why? Why do you love me?

"Can I come in?" he said before quickly adding, "Just for a few minutes. I want to talk to you…" his words trickled to a stop when she didn't move aside, the grin on his face falling away into a look of pained embarrassment. "Okay… I'm sorry I woke you." he nodded, taking a step back, followed by another. "I guess I'll see you at work then—"

"Wait," she said, angling her head out the window. Moving back to sit on her bed, she set the multi-tool aside while he boosted himself onto her windowsill and shimmied his way in. Something he'd done a dozen times over the past few months. So why did this time feel different?

"When Dale said you'd gone to see your mom, I didn't expect to see you today," she said quietly, while he shut and latched the window.

"Just a day trip," Tommy said, turning to look at her, offering her another smile. "I needed to ask her for something before she left for her residency." He didn't offer any further explanation. For some reason it irritated her.

She looked at the clock on her nightstand. It was after midnight. "Tommy, I've got a lot to do in the morning..."

"I know," he said, dropping onto the floor, he sat in front of where she sat on the bed. "But this is important... the other night, I thought about what you asked me. Thought about it all the way home." He crossed his long legs in front of him, looking up at her. "Why I love you. Actually, I can't stop thinking about it—I've been trying to find the answer you'd want. One that'll make you happy."

She sat forward, bracing her elbows on her knees. "Tommy, that's not why I—"

"Just listen," he said, looking over his shoulder for a moment at the toddlers asleep in the bed a few feet away. "Somewhere around yesterday afternoon, I realized that there isn't a right answer. I can't explain why I love you... I just do." He turned back to look at her, and her breath caught in her chest. "I love how dedicated you are to Jason and Riley. How hard you work. I love how; no matter how many times you get knocked down, you keep getting up—"

He pulled his hand from the pocket of his hoodie and opened his fist, showing her a soft leather pouch. "And instead of pushing you away I should do everything I can to make sure you stay right where you are. With me." He reached for her hand and held it, emptying the contents of the pouch into it. A silver band, inlaid with lapis. "Will you marry me?"

She knew without asking that this was what he'd gone to see his mother for. This was her ring. The one given to her by his father... the floorboards outside her bedroom creaked, moaning so softly that for a second, she was able convince herself that she'd imagined it. But she hadn't imagined it... someone was standing outside her bedroom, listening. Pete. It had to be. He must've come home while she was sleeping.

She looked up at him, shaking her head. "I can't. I can't Tommy..."

The smile on his face faded away, his hand falling from hers. In the hall, the floorboards creaked again, this time footsteps moving toward the kitchen. A second later, the front door open before slamming shut.

"I'm leaving Jessup," she said it in a rush, not sure how much time she had. Reaching out, she caught the hand he'd pulled from hers. "I can't stay here anymore—" Tears clogged her throat and sinuses. "I have to leave, so I can't..."

"I'll go with you." He said it like it was the easiest thing in the world—leaving your entire life behind. Starting a new one. For them, maybe it would be. "I'll go with you." He leveled himself up onto his knees, cupping his hands around hers. "I love you, Melissa—I love you and I'll go any—"

"Okay." She breathed the word, nodding her head, pressing the ring into his hand. "Yes, I'll marry you, Tommy." He leaned into her, kissing her while he slipped the ring onto her finger. The moment she felt its weight on her hand, she knew it was right. That she belonged with Tommy—and that everything would be okay, as long as they were together.

THIRTEEN

THIS WASN'T HAPPENING.

He refused to believe it. What he was seeing couldn't be real. It wasn't possible.

Friday night, she'd left Onewolf standing on the sidewalk, on the verge of breaking up with him. Now that half-breed cocksucker was on bended *fucking* knee, cheap ring in hand.

And she was saying yes.

He jumped when the cold tip of the blade he held touched the corner of his eye, causing a momentary slice of pain. He hadn't even been aware of lifting it to his face. That's how much this upset him. How wrong it was. He'd been on the verge of stabbing out his own eyes because this was wrong. She didn't belong to Onewolf. She belonged to him.

Mine.

His head hurt. A sudden, constant drumming. Like someone was trying to kick in the back of his skull. He dropped the knife to his side, his hand flexing and tightening around its handle. Framed by the window, he watched the half-breed slip the ring on Melissa's finger. Lean in to kiss her. The way she wound her arms around his neck. Let him push her back onto the bed...

He would sit in the diner and watch them. The truckers and the locals. The way they watched her. He knew what they were thinking—what they wanted to do to her. The thought of any one of them putting their hands on her made him so sick with rage he nearly blacked out. That feeling was nothing compared to what he was feeling now.

Standing in front of her window, watching while she let that dirty half-breed shove his tongue in her mouth, he still couldn't believe what he was seeing but there it was and the sight of it nearly killed him.

What nearly drove him from the dense cover of trees that hid him, what nearly had him diving through her window and stabbing that fucking asshole in the neck was that even though the sight of her betrayal enraged him, he still loved her. Still wanted her.

The love fed his rage. His rage poisoned his blood and his blood sang, a high pitched keening that nearly forced its way through his lips. Instead of letting it loose, he swallowed it—the heat of it scorched his throat. It tasted like ashes.

He wasn't sure how long he stood there, watching them. Unsure of how many times or ways he killed the half-breed in his mind but when the window finally slid open and Onewolf dropped onto the ground outside, he was ready.

From where he stood, hidden in the trees, he could see Melissa lean out the window, reaching for Tommy, pulling him to her for a last kiss. In the light of her bedroom, he could see the plain silver band glinting on her finger. She said something and the cocksucker smiled, kissing her again before he turned and headed for the trees.

Straight for him.

He didn't move. Barely breathed, holding the knife close to his side. Waiting. Willing him closer, imagined pulling him into the dark of the trees. Plunging his knife into Onewolf's gut. Opening him up like a deer, spilling his intestines onto his cheap, worn shoes.

Beyond his prey he could still see Melissa, standing in the window. Watching Onewolf walk away. She wasn't smiling anymore. She looked worried. Like she knew what waited for her lover in the dark. Suddenly, her gaze shifted and seemed to land right on him.

Onewolf walked past him—not more than ten feet away from where he stood—with a stupid-ass grin on his face, heading deeper into the woods instead of toward the front of the trailer park. He thought he'd won. That Melissa was his. That he was going to live long enough to take what didn't belong to him.

He waited a bit longer, letting Onewolf gain enough distance between them that he didn't realize he was being stalked. He watched Melissa close her window before moving the sheet that covered it back into place. That was his cue to move.

Flicking his knife closed, he stowed it in the pocket of his jacket and started walking in the direction Onewolf had gone. He wasn't afraid of being heard or seen. Not in these woods. Not by Onewolf. Lots of people hung out here. Drinking. Getting high. Getting laid. But it was Sunday night. Tonight, no one else was around to see. It was just him and the guy he was going to kill.

Stooping, he picked up a rock the size of a softball. He kept walking, weaving through the trees, every stride bringing him closer and closer to Onewolf.

They were about to break through the trees and onto the highway just beyond them. He was close enough to throw the rock and make his mark but he didn't want to throw it. He wanted to heave it into that half-breed cocksucker's face so he called out to him, urging him to turn around. "Hey, Tomahawk," he said, his voice slightly raised. Just enough to stop Onewolf in his tracks. Giving him a chance to close the distance between them.

He swung hard, clipping him in the back of the head before he could fully turn around. Onewolf went down hard, the back of his skull crumpling under the weight of the rock in his fist. He dropped the rock and reached into his pocket, closing his hand around the knife he kept there. Using the toe of his shoe, he turn him over, smiling at the way his arm flopped over to the side when he rolled him. Blood seeped into the ground beneath his head, a growing pool that soaked the dirt, staining it black. For a second he was sure he'd killed him. That he was already dead and that he wouldn't get the chance to stab the life out of him.

He hunkered down, staring down at him. "Hey, you cocksuckin' piece of shit," he said, giving him a three-fingered tap on his cheek. Onewolf moaned in response but didn't open his eyes. "Hey, *look at me.*" He leaned down into his face while he worked the blade of his folding K-BAR away from its handle.

Unable to wait, he lifted Onewolf's sweatshirt, positioning the tip of his knife against his exposed stomach. Onewolf's eyelids fluttered but didn't open. "You're gonna miss the good part..." he said, driving the blade into the taunt flesh of his belly. Onewolf's eyes flew open—glassy and bright—bulging from their sockets like ping pong balls.

"That'll wake you up in the mornin'," he whooped, yanking the blade out, holding it up between then so he could see it. "She's *mine,*" he said quietly. "*Mine...*" he drove the knife in again and again, each thrust punctuated with the word he muttered over and over.

Mine.

He didn't know how many times he stabbed him. Until he stopped making noise. Until he stopped moving and his breaths were few and far between. Sitting back, he wiped a shaking arm across his face, dragging blood and dirt across his mouth.

Sometimes a plan needs time to build. To take shape. Sometimes it needs room to grow... and sometimes it springs forth, fully formed. Sometimes he just *knew* what he was supposed to do—like now.

He dragged his knife across the front of Onewolf's sweatshirt, using it to clean the blade before pulling it from his limp body. He put it on, storing his knife in its pocket. Next, he stripped Onewolf's shoes and jeans off before dragging him through the trees to the road just ahead.

He dumped Onewolf there, tossing his shoes and jeans into the trees before heading back the way he'd come without a backward glance. Onewolf was a half-Apache fry cook in a town full of racist rednecks. Finding him naked, stabbed to death on the side of the highway behind the trailer park wasn't going to shock anyone. The Chief would call it a hate crime, shake his head, and file it away as *unsolved* without even bothering to call his mama.

He stopped walking long enough to pull the hood of his borrowed sweatshirt up over his head. It was deep, concealing his face. Perfect.

He could see the outline of Melissa's trailer in the moonlight. Her window was dark but it didn't matter. He imagined her, waiting in the darkness.

For him.

FOURTEEN

MELISSA ROLLED OVER AND looked at her alarm clock. Tommy'd been gone for nearly an hour. The rest of the trailer was quiet, except of the music coming from her mother's room. No other sounds. No cigarette smoke drifting down the hall. Pete had left and stayed gone.

At least for now.

Holding her hand up in front of her, she looked at the ring Tommy put there. They were leaving tomorrow, as soon as the bank opened. They'd decided on California because neither of them had seen the ocean. She imagined Jason and Riley playing in the sand. Splashing in the brisk sea water. Feeding the gulls. Life was going to be good. She and Tommy would get jobs. It would be tough at first but with the six grand she'd saved up, they would have a good start. They'd make it. They'd be happy.

She tried not to think about her grandmother. How heartbroken she'd be. She'd call her as soon as they were settled. Maybe she'd follow them. They could all live together. Maybe they'd find a place close to the beach—

Someone was tapping on her window again but instead of scaring her, this time the sound made her smile. The last thing she'd said to Tommy had been, "*Stay.*"

"We've got plenty of time for that later." He levered himself up to her for one last kiss. "Get some sleep," he said before he headed into the trees.

He came back.

She sat up, swinging her legs over the side of her bed, to let Tommy back in. Standing, she turned toward the window, smiling at the figure a few feet away, outlined by moonlight against the thin sheet that covered the glass between them. She moved the sheet aside just as he reached out and tapped again, the smile on her face wavering.

It was not Tommy at her window.

The figure outside her window wore Tommy's faded green Marshall University sweatshirt but something dark was smeared across the front of it. The hood was pulled up and low over his face, but even though she couldn't see past the shadow it cast, she knew it was wrong. The figure just beyond the glass was bulkier and shorter than Tommy's tall, wiry built.

A detached flicker of fear, like she was watching herself in a movie or reading it in a book, squirmed in her belly. The figure raised its hand again—*tap, tap, tap*. The finger that tapped left dark red smudges on the window when it fell away.

Blood.

Her eyes flew to the latch. She'd forgotten to lock the window.

The hand was no longer tapping. Now it was pressed against the glass, almost digging into it, as if whoever was standing outside her window was trying to touch her through the glass.

She stumbled back, tripping over clothes and the twins' diaper bag, until she was pressed against the closed bedroom door. The security chain dug into the thin skin along her spine, telling her it no longer worked to keep her safe. It had turned against her to keep her there—trapped. His hand moved, sliding the cracked window along its track, opening it slowly until there was nothing between them.

She wanted to scream—could feel the force of it crowd and push its way into a throat that was blocked and choked by fear. She had the distinct impression that the person outside her window was smiling at her. That he found her fear amusing. That he was playing with her.

She was suddenly sure that this was the man who'd broken into her room. Rifled through her hamper and stolen her underwear. Stood outside her window and watched her while he...

Run. She had to run.

Melissa turned her head toward the twins a few feet away, sleeping in a jumble of limbs. The sweet, even sound of their breathing drown out by the rushing of her

115

blood as it pounded into her arms and legs, readying her to fight. She might have time to gather them. To unlock the door and run down the hall but there wasn't enough time to do both before the man outside her open window gained access to her room and she wasn't leaving them behind. Fists clenched, Melissa turned toward the window.

The man was gone.

For a moment she stood still, staring at the empty space where only moments ago, a nightmare lurked. Sure that it *had* been a nightmare, she clung to the thought for a few moments but the comforting lie died before she could fully believe it.

The sound of knocking on the front door echoed down the hall even as she stared across the room at the window, slid open on its track. The music seeping under her door from her mother's room was turned down. Kelly had heard the knock too.

Turning toward the door, Melissa pulled at it, grabbing at the security chain but it slipped through her hands, still working against her. The knock sounded again and she opened her mouth to scream at her mother to keep the front door closed, but the second round was cut short and she heard the muffled voice of her mother talking.

Lunging across the room, she shoved the window closed, pushing the lock into place. She was at the door again, checking the locks to make sure they were secure. The talking stopped and the front door was shut, followed by the sound of her mother moving down the hall. Melissa felt relief wash through her. Her mother was with another man. She'd turned him away...

But the feeling was short lived as her ear caught the sound of heavy foot falls down the hall, stopping in front of her door. Instead of turning him away, Kelly let him inside.

FIFTEEN

HE KNOCKED LOUDLY BEFORE taking a step back, folding his hands together inside the pocket of his borrowed hoodie. Doing so reminded him of its previous owner. The fact that he was either dead or very close to dying, naked on the side of the road not more than a 100 yards away.

The thought made him smile.

Movement from inside the trailer, moments before the door was opened just a crack. Too many wives had showed up on her doorstep looking for their husbands for Kelly to be anything but cautious. The second she saw him, her entire demeanor changed. Her breasts no longer barred entry—now they were offered for the taking, her cheap blouse cut low and flimsy as she thrust them out. She cocked her hip to the side, offering a glorious side view of her ass, barely concealed by the short, tight spandex skirt she wore.

"Oh," Kelly purred, lowering the lids of her wide blue eyes as she took in the sight of him. "It's you. Been a while since you knocked… usually you just walk right in."

"I'm in the mood for something different," he said, coming toward her, letting his hand coast up her bare thigh until it was under that pitiful excuse for a skirt. She wasn't wearing underwear.

"I got a cust—" she started but winced to a stop when he dug his fingers into the junction of her thighs. Even though he knew perfectly well that she fucked other men for money, he didn't want to hear about it. "I have a guest." She corrected, fighting to keep the fear out of her voice.

A fifty-dollar bill appeared in his free hand while the other worked its fingers deep inside her. "Get rid of him," he said. Pain and pleasure streaked across her face, mixing with the fear that was always there when she was with him. It was an intoxicating combination. One that stiffened his cock instantly.

The hand he had between her legs was rough but she didn't pull away. Didn't ask him to stop. Her eyes widened slightly at the sight of the money he offered.

"Like I said, I'm in the mood for something different tonight," he said, tucking the folded bill inside her bra before he withdrew his hand and pushed past her into the kitchen.

Kelly shut the front door and walked across the kitchen, moving to pull down the skirt that had worked its way up her thighs. "Leave it," he told her and she did as he said. With a lewd look thrown over her shoulder, Kelly walked to her bedroom reveling in the feel of his eyes nailed to her naked ass.

As soon as her door clicked shut and the music was turned back on, he left the kitchen and walked down the short hallway, past the room where Motley Crew did little to drown out the sounds of sex, toward where he knew Melissa was waiting for him. Pausing briefly in the bathroom doorway he breathed deep, the smell of her shampoo and soap—peaches—still clung to the damp air.

One of her waitress uniforms hung on the back of the door and he touched it. Slid his hand up, inside the skirt, imagining she was in it.

He made his way further down the hall, his footfalls heavy and deliberate as they came to stop in front of her door. She had been there, pressed against it only minutes before and he felt her there now, could hear the sound of her breathing on the other side. She'd been wearing a thin white tank top and white cotton panties, her hair loose and tousled with sleep, eyes wide with fear. Remembering, he breathed deep again. The smell of her fear was far more intoxicating than her shampoo.

He twisted the doorknob back and forth, stirring her fear, sending the swirling scent of it his way, carried to him on the small scream she fought to stifle. He could hear her ragged breath through the door, the frightened hitch of it. She knew he was there, inches away from her and that if he wanted to, he could have her. He whispered to her, letting her know he knew she was listening—waiting for him.

Behind him, Kelly's bedroom door opened then shut. He didn't turn around to see who it was. Kelly's johns took care *not* to see each other—it made church picnics and Saturday night varsity football games much easier that way. The front door opened and shut, signaling his predecessor's exist.

With a quiet chuckle he turned away and re-traced his steps until he found himself outside Kelly's door. He pushed it open without knocking and didn't bother to close it. She was standing by the side of the bed waiting for him, Motley Crew wailing about *Girls! Girls! Girls!*, her auburn hair soft and loose, floating around her delicate shoulders.

Without a word he walked to her nightstand and turned off the radio. He wanted to make sure his Melissa heard what was about to happen.

Kelly knew how to make herself look good. That the dim lighting of her bedroom made her look ten years younger. Made her look like her daughter and she smiled sweetly. He approached her slowly, intimidating and exciting her in equal turns. He could see her fear and apprehension building with every step, at total odds with the lust that lurked in her eyes.

She was afraid. He could smell it, beneath the sour booze and cloying aroma of marijuana that clung to the air. He hadn't paid in a while—she'd stopped making him not long after he started seeing her but she was smart. The fifty he'd stuffed in her bra was enough to tell her what he wanted might be more than she was willing to give. He could see that the thought of it both frightened and excited her.

Her eyes flickered over the blood on his jeans and borrowed sweatshirt. He could see she wanted to ask what happened but he knew she wouldn't. Asking would run the risk of him telling her. Kelly was too smart to put herself at risk like that.

He looked down at the blood that covered him before offering her a lopsided grin. "I killed me a fry cook tonight." He reached up with blood-streaked hands and pulled the sweatshirt over his head, dropping it on her floor. "Bashed his skull in with a rock and then I stabbed him. A lot."

Saying nothing, Kelly reached out and traced her fingertips over his pecs, letting them drift lower, toward the button on his jeans but her hands were shaking. Fear was winning over lust. The only way to survive was to pretend she hadn't heard him and she knew it.

"Tell me what you want, baby," she cooed at him, working his pants down around his thighs, she reached her hand into the open fly of his pants to close a skilled hand around he cock. Usually he told her what to do, what to say and she did it but this time he just stared at her until she dropped her gaze. "Let me make you—"

"Don't touch me," he growled at her, closing a bloodied hand around the back of her neck, pulling her away from him. He piloted her toward the bed, shoving her onto it, ass in the air. Yanking her skirt up, he found white cotton panties.

This was the only thing about the game that stayed the same. The only constant that was required of her when they were together. He ran his hand over them gently—almost reverently and she seemed to relax. The fear abated. But it wouldn't last. He'd make sure of it.

Reaching into the pocket of his jeans he pulled out his knife, flicking it open. Hearing the sound, Kelly went still and stiff. "What was that?" she said, her face mashed against the well-used sheets of her bed. "Please don't..."

He ran the tip of it along the inside of her thigh, making the narrowest of cuts—a thin red line that stretched from knee to cleft. The knife was a new addition to their game, one he'd considered regularly but never had the guts to introduce. Until now. Seeing the red ribbon of blood welling against the pale skin of her thigh added an edge to his arousal. One he hadn't expected.

"I don't care about what you did to that kid. I swear I won't tell—" Kelly tried to raise her head but the iron grip he had on her neck kept her face pushed into the rumpled sheets.

"Who do you belong to," he said quietly, sliding the blade between her skin and the panties she wore, working it along the curve of her thigh until it was nestled against her slit.

"You," she said, her voice quavering so bad she had to take a deep breath and start over. "I belong to you."

"That's right," he said, pressing the flat of his knife against her, dazzled by the way she transformed before his eyes. "You're mine, Melissa." One hand fisted in her hair, bringing her face up off the bed, while the other

123

twisted the knife's handle, the blade's razor edge catching against the thin cotton, slicing it cleanly in two. "You're my girl, forever."

He could smell her arousal, the heavy musk of it mixed with the drugs and fear. Could feel the heat of it as she tried to push herself against his erection. She wanted it. The fear. The pain. Kelly wanted all of it. He cut her again and she cried out as he forced himself into her. He cut her while he fucked her, the blood it brought accompanied by the fast pounding of his hips.

Again and again. Until he had to clamp a hand over her mouth to quiet her screams. Beneath her muffled wails, a single word pounded relentlessly in his brain. Sang through his blood, over and over until it fused them together. Made them one.

Mine.

SIXTEEN

WAKING STIFF AND SORE, Melissa lifted her head from her knees with a start, her eyes immediately finding the window across the room from where she sat. It was still closed and latched but there was something written on it. A single word.

SOON

She knew without having to look closer that it was written in blood. Her mother's blood.

Thinking about last night, fresh tears started to spill down her cheeks and her head began to pound an even rhythm with her heart, fast and hard.

What she'd heard last night was far uglier and repulsive than anything she'd ever listened to before. What her mother usually did behind closed doors with the men that paid her shamed and embarrassed her but last night...

She'd been pressed against the door, afraid to move, knowing that Kelly had let in whoever had been outside her window. She heard him breathing, deep and even, as if he was trying to draw her into his lungs and then suddenly the door knob rattled. Her hands flew to her mouth, smothering the scream that tried to leap through her clenched teeth.

Her breath came in short, painful gasps and she was sure her heart would stop inside her chest, without stutter or stall, as a single word was uttered.

Soon

Separated by inches, they stood pressed against the wood that divided them and she was suddenly struck with the certainty that she knew him. Whoever he was, she'd seen him smiling at the diner. He had held the door for her at the corner market. Offered her his place in line at the bank. She *knew* him... and that scared her more than anything else.

The sound of his receding footsteps had her sagging against the door with relief. Down the hall she heard Kelly's bedroom door open with a muffled bang, the rock music her mother favored absorbing the sound of it but then it was gone and the silence that engulfed her brought her a new kind of horror.

She understood instantly. She was being made to listen. There was nothing, just an ugly silence that wanted to swallow her, stretching out until her nerves were thin and tight, her eyes squeezed shut, mouth moving in soundless prayer. She heard Kelly begin to speak but before she finished her first word it was cut off. There was a scuffle—the rustled of bed sheets. Her mother's voice pitched high with fear, begging. Asking what was happening. The quiet murmur of a male voice, low and urgent.

And then Kelly started screaming. She was *screaming*, the sound filled with pain and terror. Like she was dying.

New sounds entered the fray and these sounds she knew. Covering her ears, Melissa dropped herself into the corner against the door, the grunts and moans turning her inside out—violating her. Making her feel sick and used. The sounds that assaulted her began to take shape, forming themselves into a single word, over and over.

Mine

He was speaking to her. Telling her that whatever was happening in her mother's room, whatever was being done to Kelly was meant for *her*.

Melissa wondered if the sounds would be enough for their neighbors to finally call the police, but she knew that even if someone did call, no one would come. Chief Bauer didn't bother himself with what went on where Kelly was concerned. She was allowed to turn tricks without interference but the price was that when things went wrong, she was on her own.

She thought of her bat, propped against the wall, behind the front door. To get to it, she'd have to pass by her mother's room. He'd see her. Besides, retrieving it meant leaving the twins unprotected. She could gather the twins, sneak them out the window, run to Mrs. Kirkland's. She'd let her in… she dismissed it almost as soon as the idea came to her. There was no way she'd be able to run through the woods at one o'clock in the morning with two toddlers in tow without making noise. They'd cry. Draw his attention. She was stuck, right where she was. And he knew it.

Scrambling across the floor, her hands dove under her pillow, closing over the multi-tool she'd left there. Her hands were shaking badly, so badly that she cut herself when she was finally able to wedge the knife attachment open from its handle. It was short, no longer than her finger but it was sharp. Driving herself into the corner, she pressed her back into it and waited.

It seemed to go on for hours but the glaring red numbers on her bedside clock were frozen in place. Less than a minute after the screaming started, it stopped.

The radio was clicked back on, Guns & Roses picking up where Motley Crew left off. The door was clicked shut, muffling Axel's whine and the footsteps came her way again, accompanied by a jaunty whistle.

She was sure he was coming for her but the footsteps stopped short and a few moments later light from the bathroom, weak and watery, reached for her beneath the door, brushing against her toes. She pulled herself inward, tightening the ball she crouched in. He was standing in that light, she didn't want it to touch her.

The water came on and she could hear the sounds of vigorous washing, mixed with his whistling. The water was shut off and with a snap the light was gone. She was sure the footsteps would come back for her but they receded, finding their way back the way they had come.

They did not pause at Kelly's door—whatever had been done there did not bear re-visiting.

The front door was opened then shut, signaling that it was over, the last trills of his whistling followed him out, leaving in its place a silence that was both blessed and malignant.

She moved to unlock the door but her hands stalled on the locks, fear and apprehension rooting her in place. What if he was still out there? What if he'd only pretended to leave to draw her out? If he was still out there, he would do to her far worse things than what had been done to her mother, she was sure of it. What would happen to Jason and Riley? It was a horrible choice but she made it without hesitation.

Jason and Riley were hers to protect. If she was gone they would have no one. She sank down onto the floor, as far out of reach as she could make herself...

Now she sat, staring at her window—at what was written there. She fixed her grainy eyes on the clock. It was nearly 6 AM.

The twins were babbling softly to one another, speaking a language all their own. How they managed to sleep through last night was a mystery to her. The trailer sounded like it always did before noon. Quiet. Almost normal. It halfway convinced her that whatever had happened, it wasn't as bad as she'd thought. Imagining Kelly propped up in bed with her morning cocktail, watching TV as usual, made Melissa felt better.

Standing, she dropped the multi-tool onto her night stand and unlocked the door. With a silent prayer, she pulled it open just a crack, listening for footsteps. Whistling. Any sound that would warn her she was in danger but nothing came back to her and after a few moments, she widened the crack in the doorway and stepped into the hall.

In the bathroom, there was blood in the sink. On the counter. Streaks of it covered a towel that had been folded neatly and threaded through the towel bar. Without thinking about where it had come from, Melissa mopped it up, the sight of it churning her stomach. She just wanted it gone. To keep pretending that what she'd heard last night wasn't real.

Melissa forced herself down the hall to Kelly's room. The door stood open, her eyes instantly drawn to the bed. She usually avoided this room at all costs, the purpose it served was too much for her to face but she entered it now without pause, drawn inside by the stains that covered the bed and walls.

Her mother was gone but what was left of her had turned a dark, rusty red in her absence. The only thing Kelly took pride in beside her appearance was her bed. The mattress was high quality—the sheets Egyptian cotton, a crisp white that could be easily bleached but looking at the blood-soaked tangle, Melissa knew that no amount of bleach would get rid of it. Nothing else was out of place, there were no signs of struggle. The stool that sat in front of her mother's vanity stood upright, the lamp on her nightstand was not overturned.

Melissa looked for her on the living room couch, but the room was empty. A hard ball of unease formed and settled in the pit of her stomach. She was suddenly struck with the certainty that she had to take the twins and leave—*now*.

That's when she remembered. When she put it together. The man outside her window hadn't been Tommy, she was sure of it... but he'd been wearing a similar sweatshirt. Not just similar. The same—and it had been covered in blood.

Tommy.

She wheeled around, charging down the hall, heading for her room. Stepping through her door she almost shut it before she caught movement in the corner of her eye.

Pete was sitting on her bed.

As soon as their eyes met, he shot toward her like a bullet, closing his hand around her wrist with the weight of an iron manacle. By some miracle, she managed to pull free, her hip slamming into the doorknob, nearly crippling her but she kept her feet and one of them even made it into the hall before he swung at her, his meaty fist slamming into the side of her head.

Stars exploded in her eyes and she cried out, stumbling back against the door. He grabbed her again, this time around the waist and she was too stunned to fight back when he tossed her on the bed.

She was dimly aware of the twins wailing and it was the sound of them that had her swinging and clawing, fighting for what she was sure was her life and theirs. He hit her again, slapped her hard and heavy-handed across the face with enough force to split her lip open.

She was still asleep. That had to be it. This was all one long, endless nightmare. She was still caught in it—that was the only explanation for what was happening to her now.

Reeling, she felt her wrists being bracketed and held high above her head and then he came down on her with all of his weight, driving his knee between her thighs, making room for his hips as they pushed against her, what prodded at her from between them brought her to her senses. This was not a dream. This was happening.

No. No. No. No...

"Shut up!" Pete yelled over his shoulder and Jason and Riley fell silent, nothing but snuffles and whimpers coming from them now. Turning on her, he grabbed her face, trying to make her look at him. *"Open your fucking eyes,"* he yelled at her and she smelled beer and the sour stench of the methamphetamines he favored. When she silently refused he squeezed her face even harder, digging his blunt fingers into her jaw, cutting the inside of her cheeks against her back teeth.

He shook her and screamed at her to open her eyes again and even though she thought she'd refuse, they opened of their own accord. His face was red, contorted with things that made new tears crowd the old. He held the multi-tool that Michael had left for her in his hand, the point of its knife attachment digging into the soft underside of her chin.

"Didn't I tell you? I told you when I was ready, I'd get in, didn't I?" Pete said, giving her another jab with the multi-tool. He hooked his free hand in the neck of her shirt, ripping it open. A fresh scream built in her lungs but he robbed her of it with just a few words. "If you scream again, I'll hurt 'em." The knife dug in even deeper for a moment before it was gone again, tucked into his back pocket.

Her eyes rolled in her head, trying to see around him to the twins, huddled in their crib just a few feet away. Lying perfecting still, her eyes still turned away, she endured as he snapped the thin strap of her tank. He palmed her breast, his fingers dirty and rough, squeezing and bruising, fresh humiliation digging deep.

"He won't want to marry you after I'm through with you." His words and tone matching the hate she saw in his eyes, his hand drifting further until it was tugging at the elastic waistband of her pants, pulling her underwear to the side. "No one will want you—not ever again."

Rough fingers thrust their way inside her but she didn't feel it. Her brain fractured and she felt herself float away, the shame carrying her someplace else.

Somewhere far away.

She felt her pants being ripped off. Cool air against her skin but she didn't care. She was going away. Somewhere safe. A place where she could get lost and no one would ever find her...

"Lissa." The word reached her before she could fully float away. Riley was saying her name. She sounded pitiful and small. Not at all like herself. Like she was lost. Like she knew that her big sister was going away. Leaving her behind.

Pete let go of her wrists and he levered himself upward, just enough to allow room to work his pants down around his hips. He thought she'd succumbed, that she'd given up.

He was wrong.

While he was fumbling, she pulled her knee to her chest so hard and fast she clipped herself in the chin, before hammering the heel of her foot into his groin, not once but twice, in rapid succession. Pete let out a howl before he fell to the side, clutching himself. Not wasting any time, Melissa bolted from the bed, her legs wobbling beneath her, betraying her. Making her slow. Easy to catch.

Lunging at her, Pete grabbed a handful of her hair and yanked but she kept moving and her hair came out in a painful clump even as she stumbled through the door and down the hall.

He lurched after her, only a few steps behind but she didn't stop. Didn't look, she just pushed herself across the kitchen, praying that she made it to the front door.

He closed the gap with a shove and she was suddenly thrown against the door, her hands splayed out in front of her as she sought purchase, making contact with something hard and heavy. Her baseball bat.

"I was gonna go easy on you, you little bitch," he said, his words crowded by exertion and pain. "That motherfucking ship has sail—"

Without thought or moment's hesitation, Melissa gripped the bat and rounded on Pete who stood a few feet behind her. She swung for the fences and incredibly, caught him squarely in the head, dropping him with a sickening crack.

Pete lay sprawled on the floor—a widening pool of blood beneath his broken skull. Standing over him, chest heaving as blood ran down her leg and chin, the bat slipped from her hands and clattered to the floor. She barely heard it, was still for only the space of one breath before she was running again.

Back in her room she threw on clothes grabbed randomly, pulling them on while Jason and Riley watched silently. She slung the diaper bag from shoulder to hip and picked them up, first one and then the other.

Without pausing to listen or look she was out her bedroom window less than three minutes after she'd swung the bat.

SEVENTEEN

RUN.

She didn't think about where she was going or what she was leaving behind. She just ran... but she must've known where she was going—she must have because when she burst through the doors of the Police station she knew exactly where she was and why she was there.

"Hello," she called out, banging on the desk bell with a hand that was shaky and pale. She could still feel it—the bat—her fingers wrapped around the hard length of it. The force of contact singing up her arms. Seeing it, she curled her fingers inward, making a fist.

Stupid. She was so stupid...

"*Hello,*" she yelled it, banging her fist on the counter hard enough to jostle the toddler in her arms. Incredibly, it'd been Riley who asked to be carried this time, while Jason plodded stoically alongside her. "Hell—"

Wade appeared from a back room, arms filled with file folders, one clamped in his mouth. When he saw her, he dropped the lot of it, forms and files landing at his feet in a jumbled mess. He was around the counter, standing next to her before she could blink, his hands on her shoulders turning her to give himself a better look at her face.

"What happened to you, Melissa," he said, giving her a small, frantic shake when she didn't answer. "Answer me, Melissa—who did this to you?"

"Where is he?" she said, reaching up to swipe at the dried blood on her chin. It hurt. Her whole face hurt. She could barely see out of her right eye. Her lip was fat, making it difficult to talk. "Is he here? I have to talk to him—is he here?" She didn't need to specify who *he* was. Their father. She was looking for their father.

Wade let go of her, taking a step back. "No, he and Zeke headed for Good Shepard in Marshall, about an hour ago—I got work-study until noon."

"Why are they both at Good Shepard?" She didn't care about his schedule. Why he was there. She only cared why her father *wasn't*.

"An assault victim was found on the 80 last night," he said, looking down at his own shuffling feet. "They went to take statements."

Highway 80 was the main artery that connected Dallas to Jessup. Jessup to Marshall. It ran directly behind the trailer park she lived in. Its traffic lulled her to sleep at night. Walking its shoulder home was a shortcut Tommy took all the time.

"It's Tommy, isn't it?" she said in a voice that sounded small and far away. When he didn't answer her, she reached out and gripped his sleeve. "Wade, is it Tommy?"

He looked up at her and nodded, anguish coupled with something harder, shown plainly on his face. "He the one who did this to you?"

Her breath hitched in her chest and she fumbled it, let it out in a gasp. "No." Tears spilled over her bottom lids as she shook her head. She couldn't think of Pete. What she did. Not now.

She could call her grandmother but it would take too long. Too much explaining. She'd have to tell her about Pete. About her mother... "Take me there," she said, reaching down to find Jason's waiting hand. "I need you to take me there, Wade. Right now."

Are you in trouble?

The words came to her suddenly, accompanied by a flash of memory—Michael standing over her, his hand gripped around her arm, gray eyes as still and dark as stones.

As soon as the thought of him took root, she cut it down. Michael wasn't around to help her. Not anymore, because no matter what he said or promised, in the end, he did what he always did.

He left.

"I can't just *leave*," he said, looking around the deserted station. "Someone's gotta be here to answer phones..." He looked at her and the second he did, she knew what he was thinking. Who he wanted to call. The only other

138

person either of them knew who'd help her without question.

Jed.

"Call him," she said in a tone that'd gone flat. Looking down at Jason, she smiled wide enough to open the split in her lip. It stung, fresh blood beading at her mouth. "Come on, let's sit down." She pulled him gently to the row of chairs shoved against the wall. She sat down, pulling her little brother up beside her to wait for their ride.

EIGHTEEN

SHE WATCHED THROUGH THE large, storefront window of the station while Jed and Wade installed the car seats in the back of Jed's convertible. Wade had brought them out not long after he called his friend.

"Dad... ah, the Chief likes to keep a few handy just in case he sees someone driving around town with an unbuckled kid," he'd said, looking down at the car seats. "He figures it's better to make sure the kid is safe, rather than give their parent a ticket they probably can't afford."

Melissa looked at him for a second before looking away. She didn't want to know things like that. That her father was thoughtful. That he did nice things for people. He'd never done anything like that for her. Not once.

Wade must've realized what she was thinking because he cleared his throat before carrying the seats outside to wait for Jed, leaving her alone.

Now, seats installed, they stood next to Jed's car, talking—Wade kept shooting glances in her direction even though the mirrored glass made it impossible to see her. They were talking about her. Wade probably telling Jed what had happened to her. That someone beat her up. That he thought it was Tommy who'd done it.

Thinking about it had her digging in the twins' diaper bag looking for the pack of baby wipes she kept there. Pulling a few from the pack, she scrubbed the dried blood off her face, despite the fact that it hurt so much she felt like she was peeling off her own skin.

Afterward she changed diapers and set Jason and Riley on the floor with a few books and toys she found in a basket in the corner to keep them occupied. Somewhere, behind the counter a phone kept ringing. She thought maybe she should tell Wade that someone was trying to call but she didn't move. Just sat there, dividing her attention between the twins on the floor in front of her and the pair of young men talking about her in the parking lot. After a few more minutes, Wade started across the parking lot, and she averted her gaze just as he pulled the door open.

"You ready?" Wade said, poking his head into the lobby and she lifted her gaze from the floor, aiming it his way.

She'd been ready thirty minutes ago. Instead of saying so she just stood. "Let's go, kiddos," she said, bending to lift Jason into her arms while Wade gathered Riley who instantly let out a protesting wail. "She doesn't like to be carried," she told him as they moved through the door. It

141

made her think of Michael again. The way Riley had reached for him from the front seat of her grandmother's car. She suddenly wished that it was him who was giving her a ride but he was long gone by now. Back to wherever he'd been hiding since his parents died.

Suddenly, she envied him. That made her hate him even more.

Seeing her, Jed fumbled the passenger side door of his car open, levering the seat forward so they could settle the twins into their seats. He stood there, staring at her, arms folded across his chest, looking like he'd been on his way to school before Wade called. The swaggering braggart who took great pleasure in harassing her every chance he got was gone. In his place was someone who looked nervous. Almost guilty. As soon as his gaze landed on her face, it bounced off to settle on her shoulder.

"I'll call the hospital, let the Chief know you're coming," Wade said, shutting her car door once she was inside. He leaned down to give her a reassuring smile, reaching through the open window to give her an awkward pat on her shoulder.

"Don't," she said, pretending to readjust her seatbelt when what she was really doing was trying to brush his hand away. "Don't call him." If Wade called, he'd give their father his version of the way things had happened. He'd tell him that it had been Tommy who assaulted her, making everything she told him afterward a lie. "Promise me you won't call him."

"Okay—promise." he said, nodding while he cut Jed a look. She knew what that look meant. Wade wouldn't call but that didn't mean that Jed wouldn't take it upon himself to fill her father in as soon as they got to the hospital.

Wade watched them drive away. She watched him retreat back into the station through the rear view mirror. As soon as he was gone, she looked out the window, determined to spend the entire fifty-minute car ride in silence. They made it less than thirty before Jed finally spoke up.

"I brought you some shoes."

"What?" she glanced at him, eyes narrowed on his face.

"Shoes," he said, jerking his chin at the floorboard of his car. "Wade said you ran in barefoot this morning so..."

She looked down at her feet. They were bare. Beside them a pair of pricey sandals, at least one size too small.

He chanced a quick look at her face. He looked away, color creeping up his neck. "They're my mom's."

"Thanks," she mumbled, aiming her gaze out the window.

"Who hit you?"

She looked at her own blurry refection in the passenger side window. Her eye was bruised, swollen shut from where Pete's haymaker had caught her and her lip was puffy and split, like a piece of overripe fruit. "Not Tommy, if that's what you're asking."

"I didn't ask you who didn't—I asked you who *did?*" Jed said, edged in so much righteous indignation that it had laughter bubbling on her lips. He must've realized how ridiculous he sounded, especially after the way he'd treated her, because he dropped it, choosing instead to tackle a different subject. "You might want to take that off before we get where we're goin'," he said, shooting a quick glance at the hand resting in her lap.

She didn't answer him, just bunched her hand into a fist until the smooth silver of the ring she worn bit into the web of her hand. Behind her, the twins started to fuss. They were hungry. Confused. Scared. Thinking about it, the drastic turn her life had taken in the past twelve hours, she felt tears start to prick at the back of her eyes. Things had never been good—not since she'd agreed to live with Kelly—but they'd been manageable. Survivable. Not like now.

In an instant, her life has careened so out of control, she wasn't sure she could steer herself out of the skid. She wasn't sure she could survive what came next.

She wasn't sure she wanted to.

She willed the tears away. She refused to cry in front of Jed. Instead she aimed a glare in his direction and spoke. "When was the last time you fucked my mother?" Her voice didn't sound like it belonged to her. It was pitched lower. Full of something she'd never heard there before. Rage. "Last night?"

The flush didn't creep along his neck—it erupted there, an explosion of guilt and self-loathing. "What? No..." he shook his head but didn't look at her when he spoke. "I was with Shelley last night. We had dinner with her parents and then I took her to see a movie."

She knew he was lying. He'd taken Shelley to see a movie Saturday afternoon, not last night but she didn't argue. "But you *do* see her—Kelly." It wasn't a question and she didn't phrase it like one. "You pay her for sex. Right?"

"What is this about, Melissa?" he said, finally glancing at her.

"*Right?*" Her voice climbed an octave, bouncing off the rolled up windows, adding another level to the twins' anxiety.

Jed opened his mouth before clamping it shut, his jaw tight, eyes aimed out the windshield. "What do you want me to say?" he finally said.

"I want the truth."

Jed scoffed. "The truth?" He looked at her again. "Your mom's a whore, Melissa." This time he looked mean—more like the Jed she knew. "So, yeah—I've fucked her plenty but I'm not the only one. There are lots of guys around here who have, just like there's a lot of people in this town who think your apple don't fall far from her tree."

If the twins weren't strapped into the back of his car, she would've hit him. "Fuck. You." She glared at him, biting each syllable in half. The ring on her finger cut into her clenched hand, Pete's words coming back to her.

He won't want to marry you after I'm through with you . . .

Pete didn't have to rape her to ruin her. She was already ruined. Had always been ruined, from the day she was born. She felt the fight go out of her and she slumped in her seat, leaning her forehead against the

145

window. "I'm nothing like her," she whispered, her breath puffing slightly against the cool glass of the window. Thinking that, feeling that way about her mother should make her feel guilty, because she was dead, but it didn't.

She didn't feel anything at all.

"I know that," Jed said next to her before he sighed, sounding exasperated. "I never thought that about you."

"You're a liar," she said, her tone even and low. "That's exactly what you think of me."

She slapped at him with her words and he jerked back, stung by the reminder of his own bad behavior. "Look... I'm sorry. For everything... I never know what to say to you—how to act. I usually just end up making shit worse.

"Because you love me." The words slipped out, flat and dull. No sharp edges. No accusations or blame. Love was a dangerous thing. When it went unrequited it could turn ugly. Make you do things. Make you into something you weren't supposed to be.

It took him a few seconds to answer her. "Yeah... because I love you," Jed finally said, pulling into the parking lot of the hospital. He parked in a spot reserved for law enforcement that was close to the main entrance before killing the engine. "I'll help you inside."

"You ever go into my room afterward, when I'm not there?" She said it fast, had to before she lost her nerve. "After you been to see her? Snooped around? Take my things?"

That ugly red flush again. It crept up his neck, staining his cheeks. He didn't answer her this time. He didn't have to.

"Did you do it?" she said, shifting around in her seat to fully face him. The tears were back but she didn't try to stop them this time. They slipped down her cheeks, dripping off her chin, unchecked. "Did you... hurt Tommy because of me?" *Did you kill my mother?*

"No." He said it like he meant it. Like it was true but there was something... "I was being serious about that ring," he said, casting his gaze back toward her hand. "I'd take if off if I were you. If Tomahawk isn't the asshole who went to work on your face then the last thing you need is Chief Bauer to get wind of what's going on between you and him."

Any delusions she had about Jed not knowing about the two of them were shattered. He wasn't the only one. Wade. Michael... everyone in town probably knew about her and Tommy.

That meant it could have been anyone. That no matter how badly she wanted to blame Jed for what'd happened, she couldn't. Not for sure.

She popped the car door open before jamming her feet into her pair of borrowed sandals. She stood, levering her seat up, and leaned into the back to unfasten Riley's car seat. The girl all but leapt into her arms, her little legs digging into the bruise on her hip but she didn't mind.

Shouldering the diaper bag, she shut the car door and moved to stand on the sidewalk, watching through the windshield as Jed struggled to get Jason out of his seat.

Once he had him, he joined her on the sidewalk and they moved toward the hospital without saying a word to each other

The ring Tommy gave her stayed on her finger. Where it belonged.

NINETEEN

JED TOOK HER STRAIGHT to the hospital cafeteria, installing her and the twins at a table close to the bathroom, before he hurried through the line, snatching this and that, piling it all on top of a tray before paying for it from a wad of cash he had stuffed in the front pocket of his jeans.

"Here—I figured you'd be hungry," he said, practically dumping the tray onto the table in front of her.

"I have money," she said, reaching for a plate of fruit wrapped in cellophane. "It's in the bank but I—"

"I don't want your money," he said, dragging a couple of high chairs over to the table. "I'm gonna go find the Chief; have him meet you down here." He hitched a thumb over his shoulder before burying his hands in the pockets of his letterman jacket. "There's a phone on the wall over there if you want to call your grandma or whatever."

"I was telling you the truth before, Jed," she said, suddenly desperate to make him believe her. "Tommy had nothing to do with what happened to me."

"That ain't entirely true," he said, backing away from the table. "And we both know it."

Before she could answer him, he was gone—off to find her father. To tell him that someone had beat the shit out of his illegitimate daughter. That she was waiting in the hospital cafeteria for him. Probably a lot of other things that were half true or outright suppositions.

She couldn't think about that now. Couldn't do anything about it. She focused on what she could control. She fed the twins. Called her grandmother but the phone rang and rang before she remembered that it was Monday morning—Lucy volunteered at the library on Monday mornings.

People were staring at her. At the damage done to her face. Wondering what happened. Who did it. She was embarrassed but there wasn't anything she could do about that either so she just pretended to ignore them.

"Hey, Melissa."

The voice was familiar but it didn't belong to her father. She looked up to see Zeke, her father's deputy, standing over her. As soon as he saw her face, she caught a ripple of worry, chased by something that looked a lot like anger.

"Come on," he said her, lifting her up by the arm, coaxing her out of her seat. He had her halfway to the door before she recovered enough to pull herself out of his grasp.

"I can't just leave them," she said, stopping in her tracks. She looked around. No one was looking. Everyone was very interested in their Watergate salads and rubbery pancakes which meant that even though they weren't watching, they were all paying attention. "They're babies."

Zeke cocked his head at the table. "Wait with 'em til I get back," he said and someone moved in her peripheral. Jed seemed to come out of nowhere, sitting in the chair she'd just been forced to vacate. Problem solved, Zeke continued to drag her out of the room.

Waiting in the hallway, near the elevators and away from prying eyes, was her father. As soon as Zeke saw him, he let go of her arm. "Tell me what happened," he told her. "Who did this to you?"

She bounced a look between her father and his deputy, not sure which one she should be addressing. "I—" she shook her head, settling her gaze on her father. "I want to see Tommy first."

"'Course she does." The Chief scoffed. "I ain't got time for this shit," he said, aiming his words at Zeke. "What I got is a half-dead Indian kid upstairs and no one to thank for it."

Half-dead Indian kid.

The words clenched her stomach, pushing at the fruit and toast she'd managed to choke down. It all came rushing up and she had to lock her throat against it to keep from gagging. "His name is Tommy," she said between clenched teeth. "And he isn't the one who did this to me."

Her father's jaw flexed and shook his head, his expression calling her a liar while Zeke advanced on her, closing the space between them until she could smell the stale coffee on his breath. "If not him, then who?"

The moment she told them what had happened, what she'd done, she'd be arrested and she couldn't let that happen. Not yet. "I want to see Tommy." Again, she looked past Zeke, aiming her glare and her words at her father. "Now."

The hard tone that came out of her mouth was a shock to them both. It had Zeke taking a step back before aiming an uncertain look at her father. He gave Zeke an almost imperceptible shake of his head. "That ain't gonna happen," Zeke said. "He's in ICU—no one but family and the police are allowed in." He seemed to regain his bearings because he squared his shoulders. "Now, I need you to tell me—"

She maneuvered around Zeke, closing the distance between her and her father until they were face to face. "You're gonna make it happen, *Dad*." She wielded the word like a weapon, like a slap in the face and it worked. He finally looked at her. Listening. Waiting.

She held her hand up; all but shoving the ring Tommy gave her in his face. "I'm his fiancé—that's *family*," she said. "The rest of it—what happened to me—can wait."

They stared at each other for a moment, the only sound between them, the clicking of his jaw as it clenched and unclenched. Finally he looked past her. "Take her on up. Tell the nurse I said it was okay."

Then he was gone. Down the hall and out the door. He left her there and didn't look back.

"Alright, you got your way." Zeke appear beside her. "Now, I need to know, Melissa," he said, leaning over to punch the call button for the elevator. "I need to know if this has anything to do with what happened to Tommy."

The door slid open and she stepped inside. He followed her, leaning over to punch his thumb against one of the numbered buttons. Three. Tommy was on the third floor.

"I'll tell you everything." The doors slid closed and they rode upward in silence. "As soon as I see him."

"Alright," he said as soon as the doors slid open. "Follow my lead."

ICU was a locked ward and it took a minute for them to be buzzed in. When they were, Zeke fixed a hang dog expression on his face, lifting his cowboy hat off his head as they approached the nurses' station. "So far, this is the only family belonging to Tommy Onewolf I can find." He pushed her forward a bit and the nurse behind the counter frowned up at her.

"She's his fiancé," he said before the nurse could object. "We're on the hunt for his mama but until then..." He shrugged like he didn't know what to do but the hand around her elbow tightened, silently urging her to play her part.

"Please," she said, her bottom lip quivering. She wasn't pretending. She was suddenly desperate. Her gaze wheeled around the ward, searching for some sign of him. "Please, can I see him?" She flattened her hand on the counter, putting the ring Tommy gave her on full display. "I won't cause trouble—I'll just..." her pleas tapered off when the nurse frown folded under the heavy weight of sympathy.

The nurse bounced a helpless look upward, landing it on Zeke's face before looking at her again. "How old are you?"

She felt her heart sink. "Sixteen. I'll be seventeen in October."

Her answer pulled the nurse's mouth into a hard, thin line. She looked up again and shook her head. "Zeke—"

"Chief vouched for her." He leaned in, closing the space between him and the nurse. "She's his daughter."

She's his daughter.

The words fisted around her throat and squeezed, making it impossible to breathe.

The nurse sighed, staring at them both for a moment before she gave her head a single nod. "Follow me," she said, leading them down the hall. "I've got to warn you, Miss—"

"Walker," she mumbled, following fast behind. "Melissa Walker."

Another glance, this one questioning and aimed over her head. "Okay, I've got to warn you, Miss Walker—his condition is critical." The nurse cut a quick look at Zeke who kept pace. "He's suffered significant head trauma and blood loss." She stopped in front of a closed door. "I need you—"

Melissa left the nurse behind, pushing the door open to step inside the dimly lit room. He was laying on the bed, covered by a blanket, arms on top. Tubes and wires stuck out every which way. One stuck out of his mouth, attached to a machine that pumped and sucked at evenly spaced intervals. He was pale. She'd never seen him so pale. His black hair lank and dull against the pillow. The only color on his skin were splashes of livid purple, ringed and slashed with red. Bruises. One bleeding into the next. Overlapping and crowding his lax features.

Her. This had happened to him because of her.

"Oh…" the sound escaped her and like it'd been the only thing holding her up, she sank, her knees too loose to hold her up. Someone caught her, guided her to the chair next to Tommy's bed. She sat, pressing her hand to her mouth, the silver ring on her finger cutting into her lip.

The nurse gave her a sympathetic cluck. "I'll let the doctor know you're here."

"Alright now," Zeke said as soon as she was gone. "You got what you wanted—"

"Pete Connors." She spit the words out without even bothering to look up at the man standing next to her. "He came at me this morning—said he knew about me and Tommy," she said, her voice snagging and shredding on the razor sharp pain that stabbed at her chest. "Said he'd fix it so he wouldn't want to marry me." Now she looked up at him, her eyes dry and hot. "Make it so no one decent would ever want me again."

"Pete Conners?" Zeke said, looking down at her, repeating the name like he knew who he was. "He's the one who did this to you?"

She cranked her hands into fists. Could practically feel the hard wood of the bat they'd been squeezed around only a few hours ago. "Yes."

"Did he…"

"Rape me?" She looked away from him. Settled her gaze on the still, pale form on the bed. "No."

"Where is he now?" The relief in Zeke's voice was palpable and she tried not to hear it. Not to feel it.

"I suppose he's where I left him, Zeke," she said, the corner of her mouth lifting in a humorless smile that felt both completely foreign and utterly at home on her face. "Dead, on my kitchen floor."

TWENTY

THE DOCTOR CAME IN and threw words at her while he flipped through Tommy's chart. *Acute subdural hematoma. Penetrating abdominal trauma. Critical condition. Life support.*

The last few words were the only ones Melissa understood but they all meant the same thing. She knew what the doctor was trying to tell her. What he was trying to prepare her for.

Tommy was going to die.

As soon as the thought formed in her mind, she rejected it. Pushed it away. Tommy was going to be fine. He was going to wake up and as soon as he was healed they were going to leave Jessup. Together. They were—

"Miss Walker?"

She looked up at the doctor standing over her. They hadn't been able to find Tommy's mother. She was in

New Mexico somewhere, totally unaware that her son was dying. Because of the ring he'd given her, she'd become his next of kin.

"Do you understand what I've told you?" the doctor said, a concerned look planted on his tired face.

She nodded because she was supposed to and because it was the quickest way to get him to leave. "Yes," she said, fixing her gaze on the young man in the bed in front of her. She was tired of words she didn't understand and people trying to prepare her for what they thought was inevitable. She just wanted them all to go away.

The doctor stood over her for a few more moments before nodding his head. "You should try to get some rest," he said, flipping Tommy's chart closed and placing it back in the rack at the foot of the bed. "I'll have one of the nurses call your grandmother to take you home."

"I'm not leaving." She said it in that voice she'd used on her father and Zeke earlier. The one that sounded like it belonged to someone else. The one that gave people pause. Made them look at her like she was a stranger. Like she might be dangerous.

"Miss Walker—"

She finally looked at him. "I said I'm not leaving."

"Okay…" The doctor held up his hands, took a step back like he was searching for a safe distance between them. "At least let one of the nurses take a look at your face—" He cut a quick look at Tommy. "The cut on your lip looks like it needs stitches."

He thought that Tommy was the one who did this to her. They all did. That she was some crazy, battered girlfriend, protecting her abuser. That what'd happened to Tommy was retaliation for assaulting her. Only Chief Bauer and her grandmother knew the truth.

LUCY had come not long after she'd arrived at the hospital, rapping on the door with light knuckles before she pushed the door open. When she heard her, Melissa turned toward the door to find her standing in the doorway. As soon at Lucy saw her, her smile brightened but she could see it. How heavy it was. How it sagged a bit under the weight of seeing what had happened to her. She'd blame herself. That's what she did.

"Hi, grandma," she said, her voice trembling. She felt herself starting to float away so she turned her gaze on Tommy—let the rise and fall of his chest ground her. It was the only thing that kept her here. Held her down. "How'd you find me?" It was a stupid question. One whose answer didn't really matter but her grandmother smiled at her while she slipped into the room.

"Your father called me." Lucy moved to stand beside her, next to Tommy's bed. "He told me... what happened."

"That I killed Pete." The words were flat, said without inflection. Without remorse.

It was as if she hadn't said a word. Lucy reached over and patted her hand. "He sent me to collect the twins. Wants me to talk you into coming home with me."

She didn't even answer. She just shook her head.

Lucy sighed. "That's what I thought," she said. "As stubborn as your grandfather—that man's skull was as thick as a brick."

"I killed Pete." She said it again, determined to make her grandmother hear her. "If I'd come home with you the other night. If I'd just done what you said…" Melissa tipped her head back to find Lucy looking down at her, started to look away again but her grandmother caught her chin to pin her with a quiet look.

"You didn't kill anyone," she said firmly, her old, knobby fingers digging into her jaw. "Your mama and that man ran off—that's what happened. You hear me, girl? *You didn't kill anyone.*"

Melissa nodded, her chin wagging in her grandmother's grip while she swallowed the sudden lump that formed in her throat. "Yes, ma'am," she whispered, gratefully accepting the lie being offered to her. A lie that meant her mother was still alive. That Kelly hadn't died because she was a coward.

Lucy turned her loose to smooth a work-roughened hand against her cheek. "I'll take 'em home," she said, that too bright smile back on her face. "When you're ready, say when and I'll come get you."

Then she left, taking the twins with her. Even though she didn't say it, Melissa knew what she meant by *when you're ready.* She meant when Tommy died. They all thought he was going to die. That she was being foolish and headstrong. She probably was but she wouldn't give up on him. She couldn't.

Now, out in the hall she could hear the Chief's booming voice, held low—talking with the doctor who'd just left. The doctor would tell him the same thing he'd told her. That even if he did survive, there was a significant chance that Tommy would never regain consciousness. She tuned it out. Started to count the tiny holes in the weave of Tommy's blanket. It was what she did when they started saying things she didn't want to hear, that way she looked like she was concentrating even though she wasn't listening.

"Hey."

She looked up to see Wade standing in the doorway and her gaze immediately flew to the large bay window set in the wall of Tommy's room that overlooked the nurses' station. "How'd you get in here?" she said. Beyond the window she could see her father—their father—still talking to the doctor. Now that she could see him, his voice didn't seem quite as loud. Jed stood beside him, watching her.

"Dad—the Chief—brought me in..." he lifted his arm. From the end of it dangled a worn backpack. It was hers. "Thought you could use these."

She stood to take it, pulling it open to look inside. Change of clothes. Hairbrush and shampoo. Toothbrush and toothpaste. All hers. She set it down on the chair she'd just vacated. Wade had gone to her house. Taken the time to collect her things and bring them to her. "You saw him," she said, forgetting what she'd promised her grandmother. "You saw Pete. What I did." She glanced out the window again at the Chief. "Is he here to arrest me?" She could imagine it—her father putting her in handcuffs. Taking her back to Jessup. What would happen to Jason and Riley? Who would be here for Tommy when he finally woke up?

"What would he arrest you for?" Wade said, brow furrowed slightly. "There was nothing to see."

Whether her words confused him or he was trying to convey some sort of hidden meaning, it was hard to say. "I stuck some magazines and a deck of cards in there." He turned, gripping the door handle but didn't pull. He just stood there for a moment, like he was waiting for something.

"No matter what you think of him or of me—we're family, Melissa," he finally said, offering her a quick smile over his shoulder as he passed through the open door. "And family sticks together."

TWENTY-ONE

THE NEXT THREE WEEKS crawled by, slow and cruel. Melissa met each day with the hope that this day would be the day Tommy would open his eyes and each night she would close her own, crippled by despair and the steadily growing certainty that he would never smile at her again.

Inner cranial pressure. Shunts and drains. Infections and internal bleeding. Tommy would gain ground only to lose it. He'd make progress only to slip farther away from her.

A few days after the last surgery, they removed his breathing tube. They'd done it, expecting him to die. What they didn't expect was that he'd begin to breathe on his own—which is exactly what he did.

They moved him out of ICU and into a regular room on a crowded, noisy floor with overworked nurses and frazzled doctors. They no longer saw her—she'd become part of the landscape. She was a ghost, perched on the edge of the chair by Tommy's bedside when they came in to change his fluids. A specter, drifting down the corridor, while they hurried from one patient to the next. As far as they were concerned, Tommy was already gone. To them, he'd never really been.

The physical therapist was the only one who seemed to see her. She came in and showed her range of motion exercises. How to lift and bend his arms and legs to help keep Tommy muscles from atrophying. She did it every day without fail. It was the one thing she looked forward to because it felt like preparation for the future. A future *with* Tommy instead of without. For the fifteen minutes a day that she bent and stretched his limbs, she was hopeful and it was that hope that carried her.

She had a routine. After breakfast, she'd take Tommy through his stretches. Then, she'd exercise herself, taking four laps around the busy ward. On her last lap she'd stop at the nurses' station. Retrieving one of those pink plastic pitchers, she scooped ice chips into it for Tommy's mouth. His lips had begun to chap and crack and the ice seemed to help. She filled the pitcher and grabbed a towel before hurrying back to the room Tommy shared with another patient.

She'd been gone less than fifteen minutes but as soon as she stepped through the door, she felt it—something had changed—and the feeling drove her to Tommy's bedside. The monitors that surrounded him beeped and pinged, telling her that nothing about his condition had changed but something was different. Wrong somehow.

She didn't see it at first. A scrap of paper tucked into Tommy's lax fist. The corner of it peeking out at her from the curl of his thumb. She felt something heavy, something malignant settle into her chest when she pulled on it, tugging the scrap loose. It felt like she was pulling on the pin of a grenade. Like as soon as it was free, her whole life would be destroyed.

It was a note and she read it twice before letting it flutter from her hand to rest in her lap. It was a joke. Some sort of trick.

Rumors constantly swirled in Jessup. It was impossible to stop them—in a town of less than a thousand, everyone knew everyone else's business. Who got fired. Who was sleeping around. Who spent Saturday night in the police station drunk tank. News of what'd happened to Tommy had traveled fast and blame had landed squarely on her.

She'd flirted with her mother's boyfriend—come on strong and when he responded to her obvious advances she rejected him. Angry, Pete beat her up and when Tommy found out what'd happened he'd tried to take up for her, only to get stabbed for his trouble. Rather than wait around for her to cry wolf to her daddy, Kelly and Pete lit out of town, leaving her to contend with her own mess.

Things like facts or logic never meant much to the Jessup rumor mill.

She'd heard at least a dozen versions of the same story in the past three weeks floating around the hospital. Some had her and Tommy as lovers. Some had Tommy as just a nice guy with a crush who got in over his head. Most people were angry with her for what happened. None of them would invite Tommy into their home for a glass of water, let alone Sunday dinner but that didn't matter. Most in Jessup had tolerated her at best. Simply waited for an excuse to point at her and say, *See? I knew it. I knew she was trash, just like her mother.*

Now, they finally had one.

They hated her. It made sense that someone in Jessup had been at the hospital visiting family or friends and, seeing her haunt the halls, decided to play a cruel and nasty joke on her. To scare her. Shame her.

A joke. Some sort of trick, that's all it was. Melissa retrieved the piece of paper and read it again.

LEAVE HIM OR I'LL FINISH WHAT I STARTED

This time she saw the words for what they were. Not only a warning, but a vow. A promise that curdled her stomach and filled her mouth with cotton.

The person who hurt Tommy was still out there and he'd just proved that he had no problem getting close to him. That if he wanted, he could do exactly what he'd promised. She'd been gone from his bedside less than fifteen minutes—long enough to walk around the ward a few times and grab some ice. How long had he needed to slip into Tommy's room and tuck the note into his hand? How long would he need to kill him?

The answer pushed her to her feet. Had her leaning over the bedrail so she could press a kiss against his dry lips. "I'm so sorry, Tommy," she said, digging her hand into the pitcher at his bedside. She pulled out a piece of ice and smoothed it across this mouth, watched the dry, cracked tissue absorb the moisture as if it were dying of thirst. "I love you. Whatever you hear about me, try to remember that and that you loved me too."

It was the last thing she said to him before she walked away.

TWENTY-TWO

SHE WALKED DIRECTLY TO the bank and closed her account. Nearly six thousand dollars but there was more. Including the one hundred dollars Michael had given her, she had almost three hundred dollars hidden in the wall of her closet.

She couldn't just leave it behind.

When she knocked on her grandmother's door, Lucy had been surprised to see her. Had instantly thought the worst. That Tommy had died.

"He's still alive," she said, pushing her way into the house. "But he won't be for long if I stay here." She pressed the scrap of paper into her grandmother's hand. Watched her nervously while she read it. Waited for her confused gaze to find its way from the note in her hand to her face.

And then she told her everything.

Lucy was quiet. Stone-faced and patient while she told her about the pair of underwear belonging to her that she'd found in the woods outside their trailer. About the person who hadn't been Tommy outside her bedroom window. About what she'd heard him do to her mother.

"I'm sorry," she whispered. The twins were napping and she didn't want them to wake and hear her. "I'm so sorry..."

"For what?" Lucy whispered back, her face no longer stoic. "Far as I can tell, none of this is your fault."

She was wrong but Meliss didn't argue. Instead she stood, pulling the scrap of paper from her grandma's hand. "I need to use your car." She had her license but aside from taking Kelly's car to the liquor store or walking to the bar to drive her home, she didn't have much experience. "There's something I need to get from the house."

Lucy stared up at her like she was stupid. "After what you just told me, you want me to let you go back to that place, *all by yourself?*"

"You can make it easy for me and give me your car keys," she said in the same tone she'd used on her father all those weeks ago. "Or I can just walk there. I'm going either way."

After a few moments of debate, Lucy gave her the car keys.

IT was strange, being back in Jessup. She'd been gone for only a few weeks but it felt like years. The person she'd been—the frightened girl who'd climbed out her bedroom window was gone. She'd died by inches, confined in a hospital room, watching Tommy fight a battle she'd become increasingly sure he could never win.

The girl that was left was harder. So full of sadness it seemed to seep from her pores. Despite herself, the girl she'd been before cared. She cared about what the people in this town thought of her. She wanted to make her grandmother proud. To prove to her and them that she was better than the woman she came from.

The girl she was now didn't want any of that. What they thought of her didn't matter. They stared at her from store windows. Stopped and whispered on the sidewalk as she drove past. None of it touched her. It didn't even register.

She stood on the porch for a while, staring at the front door, unsure of what she'd find when she went inside. Stuck to the door was a large, bright orange piece of paper.

An eviction notice.

It was proving harder than she thought it would, walking into that trailer. Half the town knew she was back, had known the second she crossed the county line and the other half was getting an ear full about how she was just standing on the front porch like a moron, staring at the front door. They'd say she was gutless. Scared to face the mess she'd made. Not even able to find the courage to open the front door and go inside. It was those whispers, the one she could almost *feel* that finally pushed her across the threshold.

Closing the door behind her, the interior was cast in heavy shadows. She stood in the doorway for a moment, staring at the floor.

The spot where she'd left Pete was empty, the worn linoleum scrubbed so clean she could see the floorboards beneath it in spots.

Flicking the switch next to the door—the lights wouldn't turn on. The electricity had been shut off. She had maybe twenty minutes until nightfall, which meant no time to fall apart.

Get it over with.

She walked into the kitchen. It was as she'd left it, a few dishes in the sink. Drained vodka bottles littered the counter. Empty milk jug souring in the trash can.

Not daring to open the refrigerator, she passed it and started down the hall, past her mother's room. She walked, not intending to stop but she found herself pushing the door open all the same.

There was no blood. Not a drop. Blood spatter had been scrubbed off the walls. Blood-stained sheets stripped away. Even the mattress was gone. The closet door hung open, empty. Hangers strewn across the floor. It looked as if Kelly had left in a hurry, taking only what she could carry.

But she knew better, didn't she? She knew what had really happened to her mother. That she was dead.

She could still hear her screams. The way they'd been cut off mid-wail. How she'd simply cowered in the corner, hands over her ears. Letting it happen. Choosing to preserve her own life rather than help her own mother.

It was a choice she could never take back. One she'd make again if she was forced to but not one she was proud of. The twins were safe and they would stay that way. She would kill and die, sacrifice anyone and anything to make sure of it. They were all that mattered now.

The sun was beginning to set. Starting down the dim hallway toward her bedroom, each step pulled her deeper and deeper into the dark. Unease tightened her belly and she became acutely aware that she was not alone.

She stood still and listened. She heard nothing. No creaking floorboards. No door clicking shut. But the silence felt occupied. It felt *full*.

Like something lurked in the darkness. Waiting.

She pushed forward, forcing herself to venture farther down the hall. The feeling intensified until fear stalled her footsteps, rooting her in place. Leaving her exposed.

Turning toward the bathroom door, she found it cracked just a few inches. Beyond the crack was a bottomless dark. A slice of black so perfect and dense she couldn't make herself move past it.

She saw the blood—her mother's blood—splashed on the counters, soaked into the neatly folded hand towel, and she felt her breath begin to hitch in her chest as her vision began to swim.

Stop it. Just stop it.

She was being childish. Wasting time. There was no one here. No one was waiting. She forced herself past the bathroom. Nothing reached for her from the dark. Nothing pulled her through the crack to devour her. She was alone.

Her bedroom was a shambles. The window had been smashed out. Clothes pulled out of her drawers. Dirty clothes hamper knocked over. Her belongings broken and strewn across the carpet. Beer cans and used condoms littered her bed. The unmistakable stench of urine emanating from the corner.

Someone—probably the same kids who hung out in the woods and threw loose change at her windows—had spray painted *WHORE* on the wall above her bed.

Her clothes. Her things. Suddenly, she didn't want to touch any of it. Too disgusted to be afraid, she threw open her closet door. It was empty, all her clothes pulled off their hangers.

Crouching, she peeled the paper back and stuck her hand into the hole near the floor. She half expected it to be empty but it was still there.

Pulling the zippered pouch from its hiding spot, she shoved it into the pocked of her jeans. It was the only thing she'd come for. The rest of it was trash—not even worth the effort it would take to carry it to the curb.

She decided to leave it all behind. Start fresh. Start over. Alone.

Mind made up, she was halfway across the room when the whistling started.

TWENTY-THREE

JAUNTY AND TUNELESS, IT floated down the hall, moving away from her. The sound stopped her in her tracks. Made her hesitate but only for a moment.

One second she was paralyzed, the next she was flying through the door. Down the hall. She didn't know what she was doing. She only knew she was angry. That the person who hurt Tommy was *here*. That she had to stop him. Charging down the hall into the dark, Melissa refused to think farther than that.

Stop him.

The front door was open and she headed straight for it but before she cleared the kitchen she crashed into something solid and warm. Something with arms that banded her own to her sides and hands that clamped over her mouth, leaving the scream that erupted from her throat to die, unsounded, behind clenched teeth.

"Shhh." The voice was close to her face, the breath of its single sound traveled up her neck, brushing against the fine hairs at her nape. Her eyes were popped wide but they couldn't find the light. It was full dark now and knowing that pushed her to fight. She strained against the arms that held her but her struggles were weak and her captor held her easily.

"Come on Lissa, don't be that way, I just want to talk to you."

She recognized the voice and the sound of it kicked up her escape effort but her momentum was robbed from her when she was suddenly slammed against a wall, the push causing a kitchen chair to topple over in the dark.

"I said stop, goddamn it," he said, giving her a small shake before letting her go.

"What are you doing here, Jed?" she wheezed out, pushing her hands against his chest. He was still too close. He was always too close. "Was that you, whistling?"

"What?" he said peering down at her in the dark. "Whistling?" He said it like he thought she was crazy. Like she'd imagined it. Maybe she had.

"Yes, *whistling*. I heard it, just a second ago. Someone was..." she let her words die out. She was either crazy or staring into the face of the person who killed her mother. Both scenarios put her in a dangerous place. "I thought I heard someone."

"No, I wasn't whistling..." He finally took a step back to shove his hands into his pockets, seemingly sheepish.

"I saw you pull in and... I followed you," he said quietly. "I just wanted to make sure you were okay."

He'd shoved her hard, knocking her head against the wall with enough force to put a hole in the paper-thin wall of the trailer. She looked at him, trying to see his face in the dark. Trying to read whether or not he heard the insanity of his own words.

"I'm fine, Jed." She took a steady breath, let it out slow. She needed to get out of here. Away from him. She turned to leave but he threw up an arm, bracing it against the wall to stop her retreat.

"Didn't expect you'd be comin' back here. Not after..." she couldn't be sure but she thought his gaze strayed to the side, toward the kitchen floor where she'd left Pete weeks before. Without even asking, she was suddenly sure he knew what she'd done.

"I left something here—money. I just came to get it." She shook her head in an effort to push away the panic that having him so close brought on. "Please, Jed... I have to go."

Incredibly, he dropped his arm and leaned away from her. "Back to him. To the hospital." His tone sounded heavy. Like it was somewhere she shouldn't be.

"No. I'm not going back there." She shook her head frantically as she inched her way along the wall, farther and farther away from him until she finally stood clear of him. "I'm leaving, Jed. I'm done with Tommy, okay?" she said from the open doorway, one foot on the porch, poised to run. "I'm never gonna see him again."

"You're leaving?" He sounded like the thought scared him. "Where are you gonna go?"

"Away," she said. "I'm going away."

Jed shook his head. "But—"

She didn't wait for him to answer, she just left while he stood in the dark and watched her go.

TWENTY-FOUR

AWAY. THAT'S WHAT SHE'D said.

She was leaving Jessup. Going away. What she'd meant was someplace he couldn't find her. What she didn't know was that there was no such thing as safe.

Not from him.

She'd been gone three months. Just up and vanished with those kids she insisted on carting around. Not even her grandmother seemed to know where'd she'd gone and that asshole fry cook? He didn't know either. She'd been long gone before he'd even opened his eyes.

With her gone, there'd been no reason to stick around so he'd left too. Traveled around. Wandered. Sometimes it felt like he was driving in circles but he knew what he was really doing. He was looking for Melissa.

Waitressing was about the only thing she could do so that's where he started. He hit every shithole town between Jessup and Oklahoma City looking for her. Ate in every truck stop and diner he could find, hoping to catch a glimpse. Hoping to find her. Each time he drove away empty-handed—like she'd vanished into thin air. It began to wear on him, being without her. Began to eat away at the tenuous threads of self-control that held him together.

The first time was an accident. Maybe *accident* wasn't the right word... he'd meant to kill her, that's for sure but he hadn't planned it. Not really. Like stabbing Tommy, it'd just sort of happened.

It'd been early July and her name was Jenny. She had pale blonde curls and soft pillowly breasts that lay heavy on her chest. With her upturned nose and too small mouth, she certainly wasn't the caliber of beauty he was accustomed to but then he saw her eyes. Not Melissa's blue but close enough to bring a genuine smile to his face.

He had, up until this point, ignored her but now he grinned at her while she poured his coffee. "Ya'll got any peach pie, Jenny?"

"Pie?" She jerked her head toward the revolving display case on the counter as if she'd never heard of such a thing. "Yes," she said a bit breathlessly. "We have peach pie." For some reason, she blushed.

"Why don't you shoot me a piece along with the coffee—it's my favorite," he said with a wink and like he'd goosed her, her dumpy frame was electrified, ready to jump through hoops of fire to please him.

He spoke to her, flirted with her just enough to convey interest but not enough to be noticeable to an outside observer. He showed her the face they all saw when they looked at him—handsome, cocky but ultimately harmless.

With a shy smile, Jenny handed him his check for the coffee and pie and when he brushed his thumb along the back of her hand as he took it from her, he wanted to laugh at just how easy it all was. Flipping the check over he saw that she'd written on its back.

I get off at midnight.

He made a show of reading her note before he folded it up and tucked it into his pocket. She was watching him, hopeful that her brazen behavior was about to pay off. He peeled a twenty from the wad in his pocket and dropped it on the table before he winked at her, letting her know it had. He'd be back for her.

He intentionally made her wait, pulling back into the darkened lot well after midnight, wanting to make sure that everyone was gone, that no one was left to see them together.

If she minded being left to wait, she didn't show it. Sliding into the seat next to him, she was transformed from a shy, dumpy waitress into an incessant chatter box. She talked non-stop about anything that popped into her half-empty brain as if she actually thought he cared about what she had to say. They drove aimlessly for a while, him smiling and nodding as she prattled on, all the while wondering just how heavy her eyeballs would feel in the palm of his hand.

"How about you and me find someplace quiet to park," he said, offering her a grin that held just enough *bad boy* to excite her. "I dyin' to get my hands on you."

"Big Thicket isn't too far," she squeaked out, all breathless and blushing again. "It's closed this late at night but getting in is usually easy. We could park. Look at the stars..."

He reached over and laid a hand on her thigh, let it glide upward while shooting her another wicked smile. "Sounds like a good idea to me," he said, fighting the urge to laugh when she preened beneath his gaze.

Big Thicket was a national park, so finding their way in wasn't a problem. Closed at dusk and not offering overnight camping during the week, the park's gate was unmanned, the booth deserted. Bolt cutters from his trunk took care of the padlock and chain that secured the gate and he swung it wide in the dark, careful to cut his lights before he got out of the car. It was a Tuesday—not many late night parkers on a school night but he needed to be careful.

Finding a small clearing surrounded by a thick band of trees, he killed the engine. He sat, hands wrapped around the steering wheel, while he endured the incessant flap of her jaw. She hadn't stopped talking since he'd picked her up and it was beginning to wear thin. He was waiting— not for her to shut up but for someone to knock on his window. A park ranger or maybe the police. Someone of authority, telling them to *move along*. Five minutes stretched into ten and no one came.

She was still babbling, about how her parents had kicked her out because she'd dropped out of high school and how they just didn't *understand* when he hit her in the mouth, pulling his punch at the last second, preferring to stun his prey rather than incapacitate it. The blow knocked her words back down her throat and she swallowed them along with one of her front teeth, blood dribbling down her chin as she stared at him in shock. The shock lasted only a few seconds and what replaced it was understanding coupled with acceptance and that wouldn't do.

No, it would not do at all.

Reaching across her, slow and deliberate, he opened the glove box and pulled out his hunting knife, the same one he'd used on Kelly. The same one he'd stabbed that asshole fry cook with. A double edged blade, razor sharp on one side while the other boasted the serrated teeth of a shark.

He opened it slowly, wanting her to see what was coming her way. Wanting her to read the intention in his movements. Her fear didn't smell sweet like Melissa's. It stank like defeat. She cowered in the seat, clutching her mouth, her large, round eyes bulging slightly. He wanted to slit her throat for ruining his game but then he remembered that it wasn't the fear that smelled so good, it was the hope of survival that came with it.

With his free hand he reached out and opened the car door she was pressed against and she tumbled out, ass over tea kettle, landing in the dirt outside his car.

She stared up at him with her eyes yanked wide, her ruined mouth gaping open. For a moment he thought she would simply sit there, waiting for him to kill her but then she scrambled to her knees, her eyes never leaving his face. "Time to run," he told her and it was the slap in the face she needed to finally convince her that this was *real*.

She found her feet and stumbled for the trees. He decided to be a good sport about the whole thing and waited for her to disappear into them before he followed, knife in hand, drawn by the sweet smell he'd missed so much.

The initial chase had been exhilarating, if a bit predictable. The hard huff of her breath and the loud, frantic scramble of her retreat made the business of tracking her almost embarrassingly easy.

The catch and kill was fun. She'd wailed and squirmed underneath him like a fat fish on a hook. This, he took his time with. Told her what he was doing—made her watch him while he did—but it was only afterward, when she was dead and finally quiet, that he'd been able to seduce himself into believing that he'd found her. That he'd found his Melissa. That he'd finally be able to make her his... but reality intruded too quickly and not even the weight of her eyeballs in the palm of hand had been able to cheer him up.

She was not Melissa.

"Jenny," he said, muttering her name like a curse word. "What a disappointment you've turned out to be." Even though she was dead, he stabbed her. Over and over, her limbs jerking quietly in the grass while he yanked and

183

thrust his blade into the soft, wide plank of her stomach. Yank and thrust. Yank and thrust. Again and again until the word he stabbed into her was fully formed.

LIAR

He stared at it for a while, the word he'd cut into her— admiring his handy work always made him feel better. Then he dumped a five gallon can of gas he kept in the trunk of his car on her and set her on fire.

TWENTY-FIVE

Yuma, Arizona
September ~ 1998

"DO ME A FAVOR..." Val sing-songed at her as she strolled past, hip checking her as she went. Melissa let out a soft sigh. That could only mean one thing.

"Oh, no," she said, loading glasses with ice before adding water. "I took them last time. It's your turn."

Them. It was one AM on a Saturday and the diner they worked at was the only open sit-down restaurant for fifty miles. If you were a drunk minor in Yuma, out past curfew, and you wanted pancakes, Luck's truck stop is where you ended up. She'd heard the lot of them walk in—rowdy and obnoxious—and wanted nothing to do with them.

"*Pleeeease,*" Val said, clasping her hands together and holding them under her chin. "I'll be your best friend."

"You already are my best friend." Melissa laughed, half charmed, half annoyed. "Why can't you do it?" she said, eyeballing her friend. "You got Brad Pitt sitting in your station?"

"Almost as cute and twice as sweet," Val said, laying on a lazy southern drawl. "If he tips more than fifteen percent, I might offer to have his baby."

"*Val*," she said, laughing at her friend's brazen statement. "What would your boyfriend say?"

"We've been out twice. Josh isn't my boyfriend... yet." Val voice took on a wheedling tone. "*Come on*... take the table from hell so I can flirt while I'm still young and single." She pushed out her bottom lip and fluttered her eyelashes. "Pretty please..."

She caved. "Fine, but I have to leave at two," she said, loading her tray with the waters she'd poured. "If your sister is late getting home, your mom will kill me."

"My mom loves you more than she loves Ellie and me put together—you could probably *kill* Ellie and my mom would say *oh, thank you*, Mija—*you sure you can't stay for dinner?*" Val rolled her eyes while she pulled a pie from the case on the counter.

She shot Val a look. "She's fourteen—she shouldn't be spending all her free time taking care of kids," she said over her shoulder even though if it weren't for Val's sweet kid sister, she had no idea what she'd do.

"Please." Val's laughter pushed at her back. "If she spent more time babysitting and less time running around with that group of degenerates she hangs out with, she'd be better off."

"There's nothing wrong with having a little fun," Melissa said, defending Ellie.

"You grasp the irony of your statement, right?" Val called out, leaning back to make sure her voice carried. Her friend was always telling her to loosen up. To let go. Have some fun. She didn't know how to explain to Val that *letting go* was something she didn't know how to do. Couldn't do.

When she'd left Jessup, she'd had no idea where she was going. *Away*—it was the only direction she'd thought of when she'd pulled Lucy's car out of the driveway and head out. She'd headed north for a while before shifting west. Oklahoma gave way to Kansas before she'd cut through the corner of Colorado into Wyoming.

It took her three weeks of directionless travel to realize what she was doing. She was making sure she hadn't been followed. That whoever'd hurt Tommy wouldn't find her.

She called her grandmother every day to ask about him. He'd opened his eyes and asked for her nine days after she left. Probably started hating her about five minutes later but it didn't matter. What mattered was that he was still alive and as far as she could tell, no one knew where she was.

In Wyoming she finally bought a map, spreading it out on a lumpy motel bed while the twins napped beside her. California beckoned but she resisted. That was the old plan. The one that included Tommy. A dream life she'd never be able to have. One she didn't deserve.

Why she chose Arizona, she couldn't say. Maybe because it was as close to California as she dared. Maybe because it was the last place someone would look for her. She didn't know and she didn't care. She slept in stops and starts that night with Jason and Riley huddled against her, dreaming of sharp-looking cactus and wide swathes of brown sand that pulled you under if you stood still for too long. She woke, determined despite the nightmares, and after a quick shower and a splurge breakfast of French toast and sausage, they headed south.

She'd sold the car to some college kid for cash when they got to Flagstaff and sent Lucy the money, plus a little extra, before she bought bus tickets. She wasn't crossing state lines so no one gave her a second thought when she slid the cash for two seats across the counter.

Visiting family was what she muttered when the old woman across the aisle from her had asked what was taking them to Yuma. She'd looked at the toddlers sharing a seat beside her, both clean and well-fed, and nodded her head.

"That's nice," the old woman said with an approving smile before dozing in her seat.

The rest had happened like it did in the movies. She'd stepped off the bus, greeted by a gust of hot wind that put grit in her teeth—Jason on her hip while Riley pulled on her hand, eager to move after eight hours of sharing a bus seat with her brother.

There was a *Help Wanted* sign in the window of the restaurant attached to the truck stop they'd landed in front of. Forty-five minutes later she had a job waiting tables. Two hours and a hushed conversation with a busboy named Manny later, she had a fake ID and was paying cash for six-months rent on a furnished, one-bedroom apartment in a small, family-owned complex within walking distance to her new job that didn't care about things like citizenship or credit checks, as long as you paid your rent on time.

That'd been five months ago and she'd finally started to sleep through the night. Was able to go to the grocery store and leave for work without looking over her shoulder. She'd made a home here and in Valerie Hernandez, she'd found a friend. The first real friend she'd ever had.

Now, she shot Val a withering look while she unloaded the waters on the four-top of road trippers who'd been too busy talking about *paying gigs* and the importance of *creative freedom* to look at the menu. She figured them for what they were, struggling musicians on their way to California. They'd guzzle black coffee and maybe split an order of nachos or a basket of chicken fingers before they paid their bill in pocket change, leaving her a non-existent tip.

She smiled anyway and told them she'd be back to take their order before making her way to the table from hell. She gathered snippets of information while she took their drink orders. High school kids—nearly a dozen of them—from Gila Bend who made the Friday night trek to root for their football team. A few were actual players who'd ditched the bus back to hang with friends.

"You go to Yuma high?" a voice reached up from the table, grabbing her attention. She glanced away from her order pad and frowned at the boy who'd done the talking. He was good-looking in an effortless kind of way that reminded her of Jed. Letterman jacket and clean fingernails. Arrogant smile and soft hands. The girl sitting next to him glared at her through narrowed eyes, staking claim on something she'd be crazy not to want.

It was like friggin' *Groundhog Day*.

"No." she cut her gaze away from him to fix it on the girl hanging off his jacket like a monkey. "What can I get you to drink?" She smiled sweetly at her. The girl looked like she wanted to stab her with a fork.

"Diet Coke," she said, like she was stupid for even asking.

"You?" she said, aiming reluctant attention at the boy between them.

"Root beer," he said. "My name's Andy... you sure you don't go to Yuma?"

"Positive." She tucked her order pad into the front pocket of her apron. "I'll get these right out to you," she said before she turned away.

"Wait," he called out, grabbing onto the back of her uniform. His landed squarely on her ass, stopping her in her tracks.

She turned on him, slapping his hand away as she did. "What?" she bit out, her tone hard and loud enough to stall the round of rowdy conversation that floated around the table. Now they all stared at her like she was crazy while Andy went palms up with a good natured show of teeth, meant to make him look harmless. She recognized his kind. Knew he was anything but.

"What's your name?" he said, shooting a look around the table to make sure he had everyone's attention.

She aimed a deliberate look down at the shamrock embroidered on the pocket of her uniform. Her name was stitched across the green in white, loopy cursive. "Guess they don't teach 'em how to read in Gila Bend, huh, dumbass?" she said, cutting him a dismissive look, her comment caused a ripple in the collective that watched the exchange.

"Wow..." Andy's grin faltered, going caustic at its corners. "What's your problem?"

"*My problem*?" She stepped into him, fists clenched and he shrank away from her. "My problem is I don't like my ass being grabbed by some spoiled—"

"*Okaaay*—we'll get those drinks right out for you guys," Val said, swooping in out of nowhere to pull her away from the table and she let her, glaring at the ass-grabber the whole way. "What the hell, Melissa?" she hissed at her as soon as she had her properly cornered behind the counter.

"He grabbed my ass." The words scraped out, ground against the anger piled high in her throat.

Val goggled her wide brown eyes at her and flipped her hands, suddenly impatient with her. "And how is that different from any other Friday night?"

It wasn't. *He* was. Instead of explaining, she just shook her head. "I told you I wasn't up for it," she said, shoveling ice into glasses and filling them with random soft drinks. Let *them* sort it out.

Val sighed, rubbing a hand across her forehead. "You did. I'm sorry," she said, pitching in to help. "Is everything okay?"

No. She'd talked to her grandmother today. "Everything's fine. I'm just tired." She hadn't had a day off in weeks. Usually she was happy to have the work but right now she felt thin. Stretched and pulled in every direction. Poked full of holes, like she couldn't hold onto anything worth having.

"Tommy?" Val said the name like she knew him and maybe she did. Melissa had talked about him enough. Told her new friend everything that'd happened... or almost everything. She'd left out the part about how she'd killed her mother's boyfriend. That wasn't really something you mentioned when you were trying to make friends.

She didn't answer—just nodded. When she'd talked to Lucy, she'd asked her the same questions she always did. Was Tommy okay? Did he talk about her? Did he blame her? Hate her? The answers were always the same and they never put her in a good mood.

"Why don't you go home," Val said, shooting a glance at the clock above the drink station. She still had thirty minutes left on her shift.

She felt herself bend but ended up refusing. "I can't just leave before—"

"Yes you can," Val said, shoving her toward the break room. "I can hold it down until the next shift gets here. Go home, take a bath. Get a good nights' sleep. We'll talk in the morning."

She hesitated but only for a moment before she sighed. "Okay," she said, shuffling toward the break room to retrieve her sweater. When she came out Val was nowhere to be seen so she left without saying goodbye.

She'd almost cleared the dumpster that crowded the back door when a figure stepped out of the shadows, wrapped in cigarette smoke. She stopped short, her heart slamming against her throat.

He'd found her.

"Damn girl, you alright?" a voice said as the figure stepped into the small circle of light that shined down on the dumpster. It was Manny, one of their busboy. The one who'd given her the lead on her apartment and helped her get her fake driver's license. He was scheduled to work the 2-10 AM shift.

She blew out a relieved breath, gave him what felt like a shaky smile. "I thought you quit," she said, angling an arched brow at the cigarette in his hand and he laughed. Even though he was not older than fifteen, Melissa got the feeling he'd lived a hard life. Maybe even harder than hers.

"I'm trying but it's hard," he said, taking a final drag before dropping the butt to grind it into the dirt. "You taking off?"

"Yeah," she said. It was close enough to the end of her shift that her ducking out early wouldn't raise any eyebrows. "See you tomorrow."

She moved past him, clearing the corner of the dumpster before he spoke again. "Hey, before I forget— there was some guy in here looking for you."

The words stopped her in her tracks and she turned to find Manny looking at her, a curious expression on his face. They were all curious about where she'd come from but knew better than to ask. "When? Tonight?"

"Nah, it was a few days ago..." He gave her a sheepish smile. "We were slammed so I forgot to mention it before I left." He'd been off for the past two days. This would have been the first opportunity he'd had to tell her.

"What did he look like?" she heard herself ask, her voice sounding small and far away.

"Like a white guy." Manny shrugged. "White guy hair. White guy clothes—jeans, college sweatshirt."

Her vision constricted, narrowing in on the dark that loomed behind Manny, outside the circle of light he stood in.

"What color was the sweatshirt?" she said. She could still see him, standing outside her window, face hidden, hand outstretched. Blood-smeared fingers pressed against the glass. "Was it green?"

"I don't know... maybe." He shrugged, suddenly disinterested. It wasn't the first time a customer had asked him about one of the waitresses. "Look, I should get inside," he said hiking his thumb over his shoulder. "You sure you're gonna be alright?"

She wasn't going to be alright but she smiled anyway. "I'm okay," she said, turning away from him. "Thanks, Manny," she said before she headed out into the dark.

TWENTY-SIX

HE WATCHED HER. Smiling and laughing. Joking with the other waitress who seemed to be more friend than co-worker. He found her by accident—or maybe it was fate that stepped in and showed him the way. Led him to her. Gave him a second chance. Whatever it was, it didn't matter. All that mattered was that she was here. That, after months of searching, he'd finally found her.

Watching her now, she seemed content. At ease. Comfortable—like she'd finally settled in. Like she was happy. She seemed to have forgotten all about him. About what'd happened.

And that pissed him off.

As late as it was, the restaurant was crowded. Drunk kids and down-and-out musicians. Truckers and travelers who preferred to drive at night to avoid traffic and the heat of the day. He blended in perfectly, ball cap pulled low over his face. Non-script jacket. Backpack at his feet. Just another guy passing through.

"Can I get you anything else? Coffee re-fill? Dessert?"

He looked up to find his pretty little Mexican waitress standing over him, the name *Valerie*, stitched across her uniform. She lifted his near empty plate off the table, assessing him with deep brown eyes. Too bad they weren't blue... but for her, he'd make an exception.

"More coffee'd be great, thanks." He grinned up at her, turning on the charm while she filled his cup. "Got any peach pie?"

"Peach?" she said, shaking her head, offering him a cute little frown. "Not around here... we've got apple, coconut cream, chocolate and cherry."

"Cherry it is," he said, looking up at her long and hard enough to make her blush.

"Comin' right up." She put a swish in her hips when she walked away, shooting him an over-the-shoulder smile before she disappeared behind the counter.

Melissa appeared a few moments later, carrying a tray of ice waters for the wannabe rock stars sitting in her station. He watched her chat them up for a few seconds before she turned her attention toward the large group of teenagers that'd swarmed a nearby table. Nine of them— all drunk to varying degrees. Self-absorbed assholes. The girls snubbed her while the guys fucked her with their eyes.

Home sweet home.

One of them kept trying to talk to her. Hit on her. His attention focused, he didn't notice his waitress until she was standing over him again, a wedge of bright red pie held in one hand, a can of Redi-whip in the other. "Whipped cream?" she said, the curve of her mouth offering a bit more.

He tore his eyes away from the scene that was unfolding behind her and nodded. "You readin' my mind, darlin'?"

Now she laughed. "I sure hope—"

Behind her, he watched the boy who'd been making attempts at flirting with Melissa reach out and grab her, his hand catching hold of the back of her uniform. Closing over her ass for a split second before she turned on him, eyes snapping blue fire.

"I think your girl's about to clean someone's clock." He said it like what was happening didn't effect him one way or the other. Like the guy who'd touched her hadn't just signed his own death warrant.

"Oh, shit—excuse me," Valerie said. Their flirtation forgotten, she crossed the restaurant at a near run, wrangling Melissa away from the table. Pulling her back behind the counter. When Valerie came back a few minutes later, she was alone.

He'd had plans. For her. For them. Been laying them for weeks now, ever since he'd found her. Found a place for them to be alone. Dark and quiet. A place no one would hear her scream... but they'd have to wait. He suddenly had more pressing matters to attend to.

He ate his pie. Flirted with the waitress. All the while he waited for a sign that they were finished. That they were leaving. When Melissa's friend brought them their check an hour later, he stood. Dropping enough bills on the table to cover his food plus a hefty tip, he left but he didn't go far. He waited in the parking lot for the kid to walk out of the restaurant. Watched as he and a few of his friends piled into a car and sped off. Then he followed him.

WHEN they finally pulled into a deserted gas station about an hour and a half later, he kept going. Killing his lights, he circled around, using the entrance on the other side. Parking across the lot, in the shadow of the building, he watched the dome light come on in the car as someone popped the passenger-side door open. It was him. The kid who'd grabbed Melissa's ass. He watched him lope across the parking lot, too stupid or too drunk to realize how dangerous it was to go traipsing off into a gas station bathroom by yourself so late at night. Probably both.

Too bad for him.

Reaching into the glove box, he pulled out his knife along with a pair of gloves. He hadn't used them with Jenny or Onewolf. Nothing had come of either but he knew the odds. Unless you were careful, the more you killed, the more likely you were to get caught. Getting caught now would ruin everything.

Careful to dial down his own dome light, he opened his car door and stepped out into the darkness. He strode across the parking lot, emboldened by the truth. This was *supposed* to happen. This was his destiny—she was his destiny—and nothing was going to stop him.

199

He pushed his gloved hand against the door, opening it just a bit, slipping inside. The door made noise when it closed.

"Fuck, bro... I'm wasted." He'd heard him but didn't turn around. Probably thought he was one of his buddies. He grinned—fought hard to suppress the laughter that snuck up on him. There were two stalls and a urinal. The asshole was in the furthest stall. He could see the back of his head peeking above the partition, shoulder slumped against it.

It was almost embarrassing, how easy it all was.

The door to the stall swung free—the lock probably broken. He pushed at it, letting it swing into the back of the asshole's legs, knocking him off balance and he reached out to catch himself. "Quit being a dick," the kid slurred at him, pushing the door back at him with his shoulder. About twenty yards away he could hear the rest of them laughing and joking, the radio turned up so loud there was no way they could possibly hear what was going on outside the car.

He pushed again, this time hard enough to send his prey into the wall, sprawled against the toilet. "*What the fuck's your prob—*"

He gripped the back of his letterman jacket and spun him around, shoving at him until he was stuck between the wall and toilet. "What's your name?" he said, face pushed so close he could smell chicken wings and beer on his breath.

"What?" The asshole breathed more beer fumes in his face, the word pushed out on a panicked huff, gaze suddenly clear.

"Your. *Name.*" He brought his knife up, pressing it into the tender flesh just beneath his eye. "What is it?"

"And—Andy... I'm Andy. Andy Shepard." he stuttered it out, his face and the shoulder he gripped stone-still while the lower half of him jerked and twisted. He looked down to see that his query's foot was stuck in the toilet bowl, pants wet and twisted up around his ankles.

It was too much. He started to laugh, big gaffs pushed out so hard he had to lean against the asshole to keep himself upright. "Oh, Jesus..." he said, finally managing to straighten himself, putting enough pressure on the tip of the knife to push through flesh. To draw blood. "Andy the Asshole." He nodded. Letting his laughter die away, he pulled the blade away from the kid's eye and smiled. "I like it."

In a swift move born from years of practice, he drove his knife in deep—a single upward thrust that instantly punctured the asshole's lung—robbing him of his ability to scream for help. The things he killed, most of them hadn't been human but they still made noise. Killing quiet was something he'd had to learn.

He let Andy fall to the floor, blood pouring from the single wound. Face mashed against the dirty tile. Foot still stuck in the toilet.

"Someone needed to teach you some manners, Andy. You can't just go around touchin' what don't belong to you," he said.

"*Ssss... Ssss...*"

"What's that?" He hunkered down next to him, head cocked.

"*Ssss... Ssss...*" Andy the Asshole said again, sounding like someone had let the air out of his tires. It took him a few seconds to realize what he was doing.

He was trying to say *sorry*.

"It's alright—I accept your apology," he said, reaching out to clap the kid on the shoulder. Then he stepped on his forearm, pinning it to the floor.

Wrapping his hand around the kid's wrist he gave it a jerk, snapping it in two. He used the serrated edge of his knife to hack through the meat of his arm, separating it from the rest of his body.

Twin pools of blood merged into one, surrounding his boot. He straightened from the crouch he was in and reached over to pull a paper towel from the machine next to the sink. He wiped his knife clean while in the parking lot, loud music blared. Children, playing at being adults, laughing and clowning. Waiting for their friend while seconds ticked by. Sooner or later, one of them would come looking for him.

He dropped the severed limb into the trashcan by the door before gathering up the liner and knotting its top. Slinging it over his shoulder, Andy's hand slapped against his back—congratulating him on another job well done.

TWENTY-SEVEN

SUNDAY AND MONDAY WERE her days off and for once, she didn't offer to work. She took the twins to the park. Went to the grocery store and cleaned their apartment. Bought a sewing machine at a yard sale for fifteen dollars—Val's mom was going to teach her to sew. Hand sewing—something Lucy had taught her years ago—was breeze but time consuming. Learning how to use a machine was something she'd always wanted to do.

"She never offered to teach me," Val grumbled, stabbing her fork into the chicken salad she'd built herself from the all-you-can-eat salad bar. It was Tuesday and she was back at work, feeling more like herself that she had in months.

"She's afraid to. You can't even operate the washing machine by yourself," she laughed, dipping an onion ring in ketchup before biting it in half. "The last time you did, you flooded the entire laundry room."

"That stupid machine was broken," Val said in an indignant tone, at total odds with the grin that kept creeping up on her face.

They were in the break room at Luck's, taking advantage of the thirty-minute lunch and one free meal they got per shift. It was almost time to go back to work.

Before she could answer, Manny popped his head in. "Someone's here to see you," he said. He was looking directly at her.

"Me?" she said, dropping the other half of her onion ring. She thought about the man Manny had told her about. The one who'd been looking for her. "Is it—"

He shook his head, answering her before she could even ask. "It's a cop."

A police officer. Here. To see her.

She looked at Val, her stomach squeezing around the BLT and onion rings she'd just eaten, and instantly felt ill. What if it was her father? What if he'd finally come to arrest her for what she'd done to Pete?

As soon as she thought it, she realized how ridiculous it sounded. Her father couldn't arrest her. Not here. But she was a murderer. She'd kidnapped her siblings and taken them across state lines. All it would take was a five minute phone call from her father and she'd be in handcuffs within the hour.

Manny must've read the look on her face because he frowned. "I'm gonna tell him you left already—"

"No." She stood, shaking her head. "No—don't do that. Don't lie for me," she said, as she moved. She could feel Val's questioning stare push her through the door.

SHE pegged the officer the moment she stepped into the dining room and he was definitely not her father. Not a uniform officer either. This man was a detective. Young, maybe in his early thirties—Hispanic. Good-looking in a prize-fighter sort of way. Thick neck. Cauliflower ear. Crooked nose. Calculating gaze. He zeroed in on her the moment she pushed through the kitchen door, offering her a smile meant to calm her. No one liked having police officers looking for them. Especially around here.

"Miss Randolph?" He half stood from the stool he was sitting on at the counter and she nodded. She'd purchased a fake ID and social security card months ago from a woman in her complex whose cousin worked at the DMV. The undocumented workers in the area used them to prove citizenship and work status. She used them to stay hidden.

"Yes, is there something I can help you with?"

He gave her another smile even though the first one hadn't worked. This one didn't work either. "My name is Will Santos—I'm a detective with the Yuma police department." He reached into the suit jacket he wore despite the warm weather and pulled out his badge. "Mind if I ask you a few questions?"

"Detective?" That much she knew but she played it safe—and dumb. "What kind of detective?" Melissa

Randolph was nineteen—an adult. Fair game as far as police questioning goes.

Instead of answering her, he asked a question of his own. "Were you here, early morning of the twenty-sixth, around one AM?"

"Yes—I worked until two AM." Lying was useless. He could easily obtain her schedule from the manager. He probably already had. "Detective of what?"

"You waited on a large party of teenagers." He pressed on as if she hadn't said a word. "One of them was Andy Shepard."

My name is Andy...

Arrogant smile and soft hands. "Yes, I remember him. He grabbed my ass." She pressed her hands flat against the counter and leaned in. "And I'm not answering one more question until you answer mine."

"Fair enough," he said on a short chuckle and handed her a business card.

Det. William Santos
Yuma Police Department
Robbery/Homicide

Homicide.

Her eyes stuck to the word. She couldn't look away. Suddenly, her arms ached. Her elbow joints singing with the impact of the bat against Pete's skull. The crack of it—like an egg—rang in her ears. The detective was talking to her; she forced herself to look up. To focus.

"—finish your shift. According to Luck's corporate office, you clocked out nearly thirty minutes early that night," he said, proving her right. He had checked up on her before coming here.

"I have two toddlers at home, Detective—when the opportunity to leave early presents itself, I take it," she told him, slipping the card he gave her into her apron pocket so that she'd stop staring at it. "Is this Andy saying I stole something from him? Is that what this is about?" She played dumb again, playing up the *robbery* in robbery/homicide.

Detective Santos sat back in his stool, crossing his arms over his chest, to watch her for a moment, probably deciding how much to tell her. "Andy Shepard was found dead in a gas station restroom about ninety miles from here." He leaned his elbows against the counter. "The investigation is a coordinated effort between the county sheriff's office and the PDs involved. Witness statements put him and his friends here directly before his death and they all say that you were their waitress." He smiled at her again. Still wasn't working. "I'm just trying to narrow down the timeline. Figure out what happened to him."

He was dead. Andy was dead.

"They came in around one AM—twelve of them. From some of their letterman's jackets, I gathered that they drove here from a neighboring town to attend the football game at Yuma high," she said, deciding to play it straight. She had nothing to hide. Not about this. "While I was taking their drink order, this boy started to flirt with me—asked me where I went to school. My name." She sighed. "I'd had a long day and wasn't in the mood so I was short with him. When I turned to leave, he grabbed my ass. I didn't like it. I got upset and my co-worker stepped in and offered to finish serving the table while I went home early. That's all I know."

"A handsome football player flirted with you and you didn't like it?" He was baiting her now, she could see it. "What's not to like?"

"I've got two kids, Detective," she said, suddenly feeling as jaded and weary as she hoped she sounded. "In my experience, handsome football players are nothing but trouble."

Detective Santos leveled his gaze at her face before nodding. "Yeah, I suppose so," he said before he stood and slid on a pair of sunglasses. "If I have any more questions, I'll be in touch... and if you can think of anything else, give me a call."

She had a question of her own and she asked it before he could turn away from the counter. "What happened to him? Andy... how did he die?"

She could feel the detective watching her from behind the dark lenses of his sunglasses. He'd been waiting for her to ask. Hoping that she would so that he could gage her reaction when he told her. "Someone attacked him while he was in a gas station bathroom. Stabbed him. Punctured his left lung.... kid bled to death but it took a few minutes. Long enough for him to know what was happening to him. That he was dying."

For a moment, Tommy lay in front of her, tubes and wire sticking out of him. Skin as pale and bloodless as ash. She shook her head. She didn't want to hear anymore. "I'm sorry, Detective. I wish I could—"

He spoke over her like she hadn't said a word. "The thing is, whoever did it had to have been following him. Had to have known he was in that bathroom and that he was alone. They targeted him." He cocked his head and smiled. This time he wasn't trying to put her at ease. "Whoever it was, he did something to piss them off. After they stabbed him, they severed his hand at the wrist and took it with them when they left."

TWENTY-EIGHT

DETECTIVE SANTOS' CARD SAT in her apron pocket for almost a week. Five days of waiting for him to come back. He'd undoubtedly checked on her. While she'd been assured that the forged birth certificate and social security card she'd purchased would hold under a routine background check, she didn't feel like putting it to the test.

Whoever it was, he did something to piss them off. After they stabbed him, they severed his hand at the wrist and took it with them when they left…

Melissa's fingers brushed against the card the detective gave her every time she reached for her order pad or tucked a tip into her pocket. It felt like guilt. Every graze an accusation. Andy Shepard was dead because of her. She was certain of it.

That morning, Val had knocked on her door, ready for work. "Well," she said, helping her usher Jason and Riley across the courtyard to the apartment she shared with her mother and little sister. "Did you hear anything?" She'd told her friend everything Detective Santos had said the second he left. Val was nearly as worried as she was.

"No," she said, shaking her head while she pushed the door to Val's apartment open. The warm scent of fresh tortillas enveloped her. "Good morning, Mrs. Hernandez," she called out, telling her friend she didn't want to talk about it. Not here.

"Good morning, *Mija*," Amelia called to her from the tiny kitchen. She came out a few moments later, wiping her hands on a dish towel. "Where are my babies?" she said, dropping a kiss on her cheek before breezing past her. Seeing the twins, she hurried over to them, bending to give them noisy, wet kisses and they giggled. Looking up at her and Val she made a shooing motion with her dish towel. "*Vamos*, or you'll be late again."

Every morning she worked it was the same. She'd bring the twins to Mrs. Hernandez and she'd spoil them all day. After dinner, Val's little sister, Ellie, would walk them home, bathe them and put them to bed before doing her homework while waiting for her to get off work. It was a system that worked well. One she felt thankful for every day.

"Okay, okay..." she grabbed Val and pulled her toward the door, made it halfway down the sidewalk before her mother called them back.

"Wait, *Mija*—you forgot your breakfast," she said, rushing at them with a stack of warm flour tortillas, wrapped in a clean dish towel.

"Mom, you know I can't eat those," Val said, eyeing the dish towel with equal parts regret and distain.

"You could," her mother sniffed at her, "If you weren't so concerned with being a size zero." She pushed the stack of tortillas into Melissa's hands. "More for you," she said, patting her on the cheek before she rushed back inside.

"I'd hate you if I didn't like you so much," Val said, while the walked, watching her rip a tortilla in half and fold it into her mouth. Thin and buttery, it practically melted on her tongue. Delicious. Being a size zero had never been a goal of hers.

"Want one," she said, opening the dish towel. "I won't tell her—I swear." She smiled when Val sighed and slid one off the stack. Every morning the same.

"What are you going to do?" Val said while she chewed. "I mean, that detective didn't seem like the type to just give up."

She forced the wad of tortilla in her mouth down her throat. Val wasn't one to just give up either. "What *can* I do?" she said, tucking the rest of them into her purse for later. "It's not like I killed him."

"Yeah but you have a pretty good idea of who did," Val said, lowering her voice once they stepped into the shadow of the restaurant, heading for the back door. "Don't you think you should tell him?"

She stopped walking. "Tell him what? That I was being stalked by some lunatic who stabbed my boyfriend and killed my mother so I *kidnapped* my siblings and took them across state lines?" Saying it out loud, it didn't sound real. Any of it. It sounded like something that happened to another person. Not to her. "I can't," she said, shaking her head. "They'll take Jason and Riley away from me." *I'd end up in prison for murder.*

"We could leave."

For a moment, she saw Tommy. Heard the easy way he'd said almost the exact same thing to her only a few months ago. He'd said it like it would be simple. Like he'd follow her anywhere. Like she was worth it. She couldn't let Val make the same mistake he did. She *wasn't* worth it. She was a magnet for pain and misery. She left death in her wake—wherever she went.

"We're not going anywhere." She looped her arm through her friend's, pulling her past the dumpster, toward the employee entrance. "This is home," she said even though she wasn't sure. It was starting to look like running was her only option.

"HE'S back."

The words jerked her hands out of her pockets, pulled her gaze up from the counter to find Valerie staring at her. "Santos. He's here..." she said, jerking her chin toward the back dining room. "He ordered food to go and asked for you so I put him back there to wait so you guys could talk."

She knew what Val wanted her to do. It was what she *should* do. Come clean. It also happened to be the one thing she *couldn't* do. Not without risking Santo's finding out about what happened to Pete. That she'd killed him.

"Okay, thanks," she said. Sweat sprung up against her palms and she wiped them on the front of her apron.

She wove her way through the sparsely populated dining room. It was ten o'clock on a Tuesday. If he was here to arrest her, he'd picked a good day—there was no one here to see it.

"Detective, is there something I can help you with?" she said, falling back on the manners that Lucy had taught her.

"Just a follow up," he said, gesturing for her to sit. He didn't even try to smile this time. She slid into the booth across from him with a sinking heart. He watched her for a few moments, sizing her up. Taking stock before he spoke again. "We found the man who killed Andy Shepard."

It wasn't what she'd been expecting. The news knocked her back in her seat, relief and trepidation all at once. "Who?" she said, knowing she shouldn't ask. That it made her sound guilty of something she didn't do but she couldn't help it. She had to know. She was sure that the name he'd give her would be one she recognized. One from her old life.

"His name is James Toliver. He was a night clerk at the gas station where Shepard's body was found," he said, leaning back in his seat to study her. She had a feeling he did that a lot. Study people. "Apparently, it was a gas station Shepard and a few of his friends had done a beer run at the weekend prior while Toliver was on duty and it cost him his job."

James Toliver. She had no idea who that was.

"He killed Andy over a beer run?" It didn't sound reasonable. It sounded crazy.

"Toliver has a history of instability and violent behavior," Santos said as it explained everything. "He'd been following Shepard for days before he finally cracked. Claims he took his hand for stealing."

"Claims?" she said, trying to understand what he was saying. "This guy confessed?"

"Sure did," Santos nodded like he couldn't believe it either. "Waltzed right into the police station this morning with the bloody paper towel he used to clean his knife."

Suddenly, Val was there with a plastic bag full of take-out boxes. "Your food's ready, detective," she said, setting the bag on the table between them.

"Thank you." Santos slid out from the booth and stood over her. "I just thought you should know. I'm sorry to have bothered you, Miss Randolph." he said with a curt nod before leaving. As soon as he was out the door, Val slid into the seat he'd just vacated.

"Tell me," she hissed at her, her eyes trained over her shoulder. Probably watching the detective's retreat. "Melissa—"

She filled her in, told her friend everything that Santos had shared with her.

"So, none of this had anything to do with you," Val said, blowing out a relieved breath. "You're okay. Everything is okay."

"I guess so."

Val was smiling so she smiled back even though it felt wrong. It wasn't okay. A boy was dead. For his family, nothing would ever be okay again. But she didn't know James Toliver. She'd never met him in her life and he'd *confessed* which meant that Andy Shepard's murder had nothing to do with her. His death was not her fault. It had all been nothing but an awful, sick coincidence.

She kept repeating it until she believed it.

TWENTY-NINE

October 1ˢᵗ, 1998

VAL WAS A HORRIBLE singer. What made her even *more* horrible was that she seemed to revel in it. Instead of embarrassing her, her total lack of tone or pitch seemed to spur her to sing louder and louder until, when they'd finally reached the blessed end of the short song she was screeching so loud and off-key that it suddenly sounded as if she were singing a solo. While strangling a cat.

Embarrassed, Melissa watched her friend push her way through the kitchen door followed by a small parade of busboys—cake in hand. She took a quick look around the restaurant at the scatter of late night customers. All of them stared at the spectacle that was Val singing. The blush on her cheeks sank deeper into her skin. She covered them with her hands but couldn't help but smile.

It was her birthday.

"Make a wish." Val placed the cake on the counter in front of her with a small flourish. She closed her eyes and did as she was told before blowing out the candles. Seventeen of them. She'd made it. A corner turned.

A smattering of claps sounded off, customers and busboys cheering her on. "What did you wish for?" Val said, hip-checking her while passing her a knife to cut the cake.

"That someone would give you singing lessons," she said and laughter followed the clapping. Val turned toward the dining room with a curtsy and blew kisses at the diners before turning back toward the counter.

"I told you not to do this, really—it's no big deal, Val." She pulled candles out of the cake for lack of anything better to do. The small cluster of busboys and dishwashers wished her a happy birthday before they drifted away, back to work.

"Like I ever listen, *Chica*," Val said with an eye roll. "So? Did you think about it?" her tone was hopeful but it faded fast when she saw the decline form on her face.

"I can't," she said, face tipped toward the cake as she slid the knife Val handed her through its middle. Rather than look up at the frustrated glare she knew her friend was sending her way, she concentrated on cutting the cake into perfect wedges. Val kept glaring until she finally gave up. "I gotta get home, Val. The twins—"

"Are fine." Val took the knife from her and lifted a piece of cake onto a plate. She'd been invited to a party at school and asked her to tag along. "They're with my mother—even *she* thinks you need to get out and have some fun," she said, forking a bite of cake into her mouth. "You *do* know what fun is, right?"

"Yes, smartass," she said with a good natured grin. "I know what fun is."

"Oh yeah? When was the last time you had any?" Val held out a forkful of cake and she took it.

She smelled it before the bite hit her tongue. Sugary and tart. Baked and buttery. Lemon pound cake. Her grandmother's recipe. "Where'd you get this?" It tasted like home. The home she'd had before Kelly had come in and ripped it all away. Simple. Safe. Before the darkness found her.

"I sure as hell didn't bake it. You're grandma overnighted it." She shook her head. "And that was a serious question. How long as it been since you've had any fun?"

Rolling the taste over her tongue, she pretended to think about it. The truth was, she'd never been to a party. Could never afford the luxury of being careless. Making mistakes.

"See—you can't even remember." Val pulled the fork back to feed herself another bite. "It's your birthday for crying out loud. You're young, gorgeous and obviously in need of a drink. Possibly several. I mean, how long has it been since you've even *seen* a boy outside the restaurant?" Val said, seconds before she winced, screwing her eyes shut against her own callousness. "Sorry... I'm a total shit."

"Don't be," she said, the taste of sweet lemons going sour in her mouth. "You're right—it's been six months. Time to move on, right?"

Val heaved a sigh. "That's not what I meant..." she stalled out, searching for the right words. "I just want you to be happy here."

Now she smiled, a genuine lift at the corners of her mouth. "I am," she said and she was. She had things here that she'd never had before. Anonymity. Freedom. Friends. If she had Tommy too, it would've been too much. Too perfect.

"But you still won't come," Valerie said and she smiled at her.

"Nope."

"Okay. I'll just call Josh and tell him to go without me." Val gave her a single nod, meant to close the subject. "We'll order pizza and finish off this cake. Paint each other's toes—"

"Oh, no you don't—you're going to that party Valerie Hernandez. This is date number three with this guy and I'm not going to be the one who ruined it," she said.

"Then come with me," Val wheedled. She was good at wheedling and Melissa felt herself start to cave for a moment before she rallied.

"Third Wheel? No thanks." She couldn't go out and pretend that her life was normal. Nothing about her life was normal. Never had been. She looked over her shoulder at the clock. It was ten PM. "He's gonna be here to get you any minute—you better go get changed."

As if on cue, Val's almost-boyfriend walked in, hand lifted in greeting. "Hey—you ready to go?"

"See—told ya so." She smiled when her friend let out a yelp. "Go, get ready. I'll ply him with baked goods," she said, pushing Val in the direction of the break room. She turned to Josh, a plated slice, held aloft. "Hey, Josh—want a piece of cake?"

THIRTY minutes and two pieces of cake later, Val emerged from the break room, looking amazing in a pair of tight jeans and a halter top the color of raspberries, her long, dark hair hanging loose and thick over her shoulders.

The second he saw her, Josh sat up, letting out a low whistle. "Totally worth the wait," he said, grinning from ear to ear.

"Down, boy," Val said, giving him a wink before she turned toward her. "Last chance..."

Melissa shook her head. "Nope. I'm gonna go home, soak in the tub and watch Conan O'Brien," she said. Her tone was firm and closed the subject.

"Fine, you big party pooper..." Val said, finally conceding defeat. "At least let one of the busboys drive you home."

"It's three blocks away. I'm perfectly fine to walk." She looked down at the uneaten cake—she'd take it home for Jason and Riley. "And I better get going. I don't like Ellie out late at night."

"You live across the courtyard," Val said, flipping her hair over her shoulder. She sounded irritable but she didn't argue anymore. "I'll call you tomorrow morning and tell you *everything*." She leaned into pinch a corner off what was left of the cake and popped it into her mouth.

"You better," she said on a laugh and blocked Valerie's fingers when they tried for a second pass. "Take her Josh, before she eats all my cake."

As soon as they were gone, she re-boxed the cake and carried it with her to the break room. She grabbed her sweater and purse from the hook and hustled out the back door before someone insisted on driving her home..

THIRTY

SHE PULLED THE LAPLES of her sweater across her chest with one hand while the other balanced the cake box. Early October was still warm in Arizona—the sweater was unnecessary but she wore it anyway. It was her grandmother's. She'd found it in the backseat of the car before she'd sold it and she put it on whenever she missed home. Today, she missed it more than she'd ever thought possible. Not the place—the people.

Her grandmother. Tommy.

She'd lost her home so she'd made another. In many ways, this one was better than the one she'd left behind. She focused on that. Not on what it had cost her but on all the ways she was fortunate. She had Jason and Riley. Friends. A steady job. This was a good life. Maybe not the one she'd thought she'd have—or even the one she wanted—but she was safe and so were the ones she left behind. She had to let that count for something.

She was only a block from the apartment complex when she felt it. The neighborhood she lived in wasn't the greatest but the people in it looked out for each other. Protected those who belonged from outsiders. The police. Immigration. People looking to cause trouble. After 6 months, she belonged... but tonight, it was quiet. No one sitting on their front stoops. No car radios blaring—not even a dog barking.

Just like that, her impossible dream shattered.

Picking up the pace, she looked around. The street was deserted. But she still felt it. That sense of *fullness* she'd had the night she left. Suddenly she was back in the hallway of their run-down trailer, staring into the thin slice of dark where her mother's killer had washed his hands.

Her legs moved faster, carrying her across the mouth of the alley when she felt a prickle. Like something with scales had slithered across her nape. Footsteps, crunching across gravel, falling into time with hers, echoed behind her. She looked over her shoulder, felt herself tumble headlong down the rabbit hole.

He was here.

The hood of his sweatshirt was up and pulled low, concealing his face, hands jammed into the front pocket. His stride, long and full of purpose. Even though his face was hidden, she knew he was smiling.

He'd found her.

A strangled sob escaped her and she bobbled the cake box. It dumped out of her hands, her leftover birthday cake instantly forgotten. She ran down the sidewalk, her legs clumsy, her breath ragged in her chest. Slow… she was too slow. He was close, so close, but she didn't look back.

She tried to run faster but knew it wouldn't be enough. *Please, please, please…*

She couldn't hear him behind her anymore. Maybe he'd given up. Even though she *knew*, hope dug deep—spurred her on. She was almost there. She could see the row of apartment mailboxes in front of her building, illuminated by the street light. She was fine, she was safe. She was going to make it—

A hand fell, hard and heavy, on her face. An arm hooked her from behind, lifted her off her feet and dragged her into the waiting dark.

Dying to know what happens next?
The story continues in Maegan Beaumont's
Award-winning novel, *Carved in Darkness...*

ONE
Yuma, Arizona
1998

WAITING WAS ALWAYS THE worse part. The sporadic stretches of time between his visits—when he came and hurt her—were the hardest torture to bear. She had no idea how long she'd been in the dark. No longer trusted herself to count the days. It'd been October first when he took her. What month it was now was impossible to figure out but if every time he raped her marked the passing of a day, every time he cut her, the passing of an hour then she'd been locked away for centuries and everyone she loved was dead and gone.

Shifting, she felt the pull of dried blood and unhealed wounds across her skin. She couldn't see them—the only kindness the darkness granted her—but she could feel them. Smell them. They were everywhere. Cuts, long and thin, ran the length of her spine. The inside of her thighs. Along the swell of her breasts. The soft flesh under her arms. The soles of her feet. The stench of old blood and infection mingled with the warm, revolting smell of the bucket she was forced to use as a toilet. She tried not to think about it. About what had been done to her body. About what she'd been forced to do to survive…

Sounds penetrated the dense folds of black that surrounded her.

Footsteps. Slow and measured.

Terror gripped her, forced movement into limbs no longer totally under her control. Lurching to her feet, she swayed beneath the almost impossible heaviness of her own body weight. She took a few shuffling steps, leaning heavily against the wall in order to stay upright.

He wanted to play.

Her hands were encased in duct tape—wrapped round and round until her fingers were fused together and rendered useless. Without working fingers, getting the door open was difficult, but not impossible. It finally swung open—step by step, she forced her legs and feet forward until she slammed into the wall opposite the door. Pressing her battered cheek against it, she dragged cleaner air into her lungs in ragged gulps.

Light glowed a dull, muted red against her lids. Instinct seized her, her brain sent the signal, tried to open her eyes even though she knew she couldn't. Her lids wouldn't budge—hadn't since she woke in the dark.

Experience told her that going right was wrong. There were stairs to the right but they led to nothing more than a locked door. He wanted to chase her. It was his favorite game. She could feel him, standing at the base of the stairs.

Staring at her.

Her heart started its frantic kicking. It bounced around her chest, tried to claw its way up her throat. Turning left, she moved legs as fast as they'd go, her shoulder hugging the wall to keep herself upright.

Footsteps echoed after her, slow at first but then faster and faster.

He was coming.

HE reached the bottom of the stairs and smiled when the door flew open. Watched her stumble across the hall and slam into the wall in front of her. He took a deep breath—pulled the sweet smell of her blood into his chest and held it.

Even at a distance, he could feel the heat of it. The way it tingled across his skin. His mouth began to water. The need to taste her was a fire in his blood. He'd fought against the burn for years. Not because he felt like what he wanted to do to her was wrong but because he *knew*.

Eventually he'd go too far and end up killing her. Killing wasn't the problem. The problem was the more he had of her, the more he tasted her, the less he was able to control himself. Every time he drew his knife across her skin, the urge to push the blade in just a little deeper grew stronger and stronger. Sooner or later, he was gonna snap. Wouldn't be able to stop himself. The thought worried him. He could feel it, circling closer and closer. Not that he didn't like killing—no, killing was fun. He'd killed lots of times. Animals—cats and rabbits mostly. A dog here and there.

Some people said animals didn't have souls but he knew that wasn't true. Felt them plenty as they wriggled free of the meat and bone that trapped them. Sometimes he had to force it out and sometimes that slippery thing seemed almost grateful to be set free. He liked it better when they put up a fight. Liked to peel back the skin—layer by layer—until the screaming thing beneath him simply... stopped.

But his Melissa was different.

There was fight in her. More than he'd bargained for—it thrilled him beyond measure. He'd had her for eighty-two days—eighty-three, if he counted today—and she hadn't given in. Hadn't wriggled free.

Not yet, anyway.

She lurched forward, her gait made slow and uneven by the drugs he kept her on. Her naked body smeared with blood he'd drawn. Covered in wounds he'd inflicted.

Beautiful. Almost too beautiful to be real. He swept his gaze over her face before they settled on her eyes and the neat row of stitches that kept them closed. He was sorry for it—not being able to see her eyes. He wanted to rip those stitches out of her lids and force her eyes open, make her look at him. Make her see him—but he couldn't. Seeing him would ruin everything.

His eyes traveled downward. The blood was freshest between her thighs. Thick and dark. Moist and warm. Seeing it killed his amusement, dried it up. The thought of nesting there—pumping himself into that slippery hole between her legs, cutting her while he did, over and over—moved him forward. He could see it. Her blood-slicked skin, marbled with his semen. His hands and cock covered in both.

Reaching into his pocket, he pulled out the KA-BAR he always carried. The knife had been a gift from his father for his twelfth birthday. If he knew what he'd been using it for, his daddy wouldn't be too happy. Thinking about it made him smile. He flicked the blade open and gripped it tight.

Looking at her always made him hungry.

He started after her, took the distance slow at first, but every inch forward pushed him harder and faster until he was nearly running. Fell on her, dragged her under and she went down swinging and screaming.

Just how he liked it.

SHE hit the floor, her skull bouncing off the unforgiving pad of concrete that had only seconds before been under her feet. Her arms swung wildly, hitting him again and again.

The sound of his laughter told her he found her efforts amusing. Anger roiled around with the terror. The scream forced its way out, nothing more than a dry croak that burned her throat as she drove the flat of her foot into something soft. He grunted in pain and let go.

Suddenly free, she rolled over, tried to crawl but couldn't. Digging her fingers into the rough floor, she pulled—dragged herself until she had nowhere to go.

Dead end.

231

Pressing herself against the wall, she drew her legs to a chest that heaved and wracked with dry, wordless sobs.

He'd recovered from whatever minor damage she'd managed to inflict, was standing over her. He wasn't laughing anymore.

She heard the jerk and snap of his belt as he yanked it off. Felt the bite and hiss of his zipper as he drew it down.

Battered knees forced themselves harder into her chest. Her swollen face buried itself against her thighs.

Please... please let me die this time. Let me go. Please—

His hand fell on her head, gripped her hair and flung her to the floor. He crouched beside her, his warm breath excited and hurried against her face and neck. Grabbing her arms, he looped his belt around her wrists, yanked them above her head. Bent them back until they felt like they'd snap in two. Her eyes rolled in her sockets. The red burn of light behind her lids went black.

Hands fell on her thighs and yanked them wide. A fierce burn, accompanied by the horrible pressure of him inside her as he rammed his hips against her—faster and faster—his grunts and moans a dull roar inside her head.

"Mine. Mine. Mine..." He muttered it over and over, each thrust accompanied by the only word she'd ever heard him say. She knew him, but every time she tried to focus on the voice behind the guttural tone, she got lost. Let herself drift away from what was happening to her until the pain and horror faded away into nothing more than shadow.

The tip of his knife sank in, dragged along her breast, skirted around the rapid, uneven rhythm of her heart but she hardly felt it. His tongue came next, flat and wet against her breast, lapping at the blood his knife had drawn. The feel of it turned her stomach—she was almost glad when he pushed the blade in further and she prayed this time he'd force it deep enough to kill her. It bumped along her ribcage, its journey made jagged and broken by each brutal thrust of his hips. The blade skated along her belly, his muttering became frenzied, almost enraged. The pounding between her thighs came even faster, even more violent.

Over. It was almost over—

The blade at her belly sank in deep, a vertical breach that stole her breath and answered her prayers.

The lift and drag of the knife being yanked from her torso set her on fire, followed by another thrust of both hips and knife. *"Mine."* This time he sank the blade in at a diagonal angle.

Lift. Drag. Thrust. *"Mine."* Diagonal.

Lift. Drag. Thrust. *"Mine."* Vertical.

It was the letter M.

Something inside her broke free and floated away. The legs she'd tried so desperately to close, even with him between them, went lax. A sudden warmth stole over her and she smiled.

She was dying. She was finally free.

HE felt for a pulse. Nothing.

Watched her gore splattered chest for the rise and fall of breathing. It was still.

He bathed her and put her in the trunk before driving toward the place he'd picked out a few weeks before. It was far from where he'd kept her, even farther from where he'd taken her. A small building appeared to the left of the road and he turned. It was a Catholic church—St. Rose of Lima. The structure was squat and brown, hunkered in the dirt it sat in, as if afraid of the wide night sky and endless desert that surrounded it.

St. Rose served a transient congregation. Mostly migrant workers that labored in the cotton and melon fields that dotted the landscape. He drove around the back of the building and killed the engine. He watched the back of the building for a few minutes to ensure it was empty.

The first time he'd ever seen her was in a church—one much different from St. Rose. It'd been a Baptist church. Tall and proud. Surrounded by trees. He'd seen her sitting in the front pew with her grandmother—her stunning face so serious, her Sunday dress clean but faded and nearly too small for her growing frame—and knew she was meant to be his. She belonged to him. Looking at her, one word pounded through his brain, over and over.

Mine.

She'd been young, too young to be alarmed when she caught him staring at her. She'd looked at him from across the aisle with the bluest eyes he'd ever seen—and smiled. Just remembering it took his breath away.

He popped the trunk and got out of the car. This time he cradled her in his arms like he was crossing the threshold with his bride. Hunkered down, he freed one of his gloved hands from his bundle and unlatched the gate to step into the tiny prayer garden behind the church.

It was nothing more than a few trees and some rosebushes planted next to a marble bench but he imagined it was paradise as he stretched his Melissa out over the bench. Kneeling beside her, he pulled a pair of cuticle scissors from his front pocket and used them to snip the sutures from her lids. As careful as he was, each pass of the scissors tore the delicate flesh. Blood leaked from the corners of her eyes and he swept it away, smearing it across her temple with his gloved thumb. After the stitches were removed he peeled them open, eager to see her beautiful blue eyes. Anticipation soured in his belly as soon as his eyes locked onto hers.

They were empty.

The blanket fell open, gave him a glimpse of naked flesh. Distracted, he moved it aside completely to give himself some more. He cupped her breast, still warm from the blanket, and fondled it—felt himself go hard at the sight and feel of her. His eyes travel downward until they found her stomach and the collection of stab wounds he'd left there. His groin began to throb and his free hand fell to it, began to stroke it through the rough fabric of his jeans.

He considered having sex with her, one last time, but the thought was fleeting, chased away by a flutter—weak and sporadic—beneath his hand. The hand on his crotch went still and he flattened the other against her chest and pressed down. Searching for the heartbeat he was sure he'd just felt, but there was nothing there. A minute passed, then two. He dropped his hand. She was gone.

He was unsure of how much time had passed but when the lone howl of a coyote cut across the desert he took it as a warning.

It was time to leave.

TWO

San Francisco, California
2013

IT WAS OCTOBER FIRST.

Sabrina rolled over and stared at the wall. She knew the date. Not because she'd checked her calendar or because the leaves on the trees outside her bedroom window were turning from green to gold.

No. It was because she hadn't been able to take a deep breath for weeks now. The feeling that someone was watching her. The long hours stretched between the setting and the rising of the sun, spent wandering her silent house, kept awake by the certainty that if she closed her eyes, she'd never be able to open them again. That was what told her what day it was.

Fifteen years ago, today, she'd been kidnapped. Held for eighty-three days. Raped. Tortured. Left for dead in a churchyard.

It was October first.

She looked at her alarm clock. It was five AM. Rolling out of bed, she made her way to the bathroom to splash cold water on her face in a vain attempt to wash away another sleepless night. Afterward, she pulled on a pair of yoga pants and a plain black T-shirt over a tank of the same color. Socks and her trusty running shoes came next. They fit her like a second skin from the countless miles they'd pounded out together. Under her bed was a shoe box. In it was her Ruger LCP .380. She strapped it to her ankle and stood, the full leg of her pants concealed it perfectly.

Jogging, down the set of exterior stairs from the attic's third-floor landing, Sabrina took the cobble stone path she laid herself around the side of the house. The rambling Victorian, situated on an over-sized lot, was a complete nightmare, defensively speaking. Too many trees and bushes offered an obstructed view from the street. Too many exterior doors and windows presented multiple points of entry. Its saving grace—the only reason she'd agreed to buy the place, was that it had a finished attic, set apart from the rest of the house, with its own entrance. As much as she loved her family, she needed her own space.

Her running partner waited on the sidewalk for her, as he did most mornings. He whined with excitement just beyond the pretty picket fence bordering her front yard. Seeing him, she pulled up short with a shake of her head.

"We can't keep meeting like this, Noodlehead. One of these days we're gonna get caught." Opening the gate, she stepped onto the sidewalk. Noodles, the neighbor's chocolate Lab, whined in response. He danced around in a tight circle at her feet before planting his rump on the cold concrete. He lifted a paw and cocked his head, his tail going a mile a minute.

"Fine, you can come but if we get caught, I'm blaming it all on you." She heaved an exaggerated sigh and grabbed his paw. He pulled his paw from her grasp and shot down the sidewalk toward the park at the end of the street.

Sabrina's feet absorbed the transfer from hard pavement to soft earth as they hit the trail winding through the woods surrounding the park. Once swallowed by the trees, Noodles ran off into the brush, his occasional happy bark sounding back to her. He must've found something fun to chase.

She opened herself up. Let her legs set a brutal pace, eating the trail with hungry strides. Forced her mind to pull free of the nightmares of just a few hours before. Her legs burned, but she didn't slow. Instead, she used the pain to sandblast the dregs of last night from her thoughts.

Footsteps pounded behind her, the sound of them almost perfectly matched to her own. The sound of them made her uneasy and she pushed herself harder. Ran a bit faster. The footsteps behind her faded for a moment then doubled, catching up with her. No more than fifteen feet now. Shifting across the trail, she hugged the tree line to give the person behind her room to pass. They didn't pass, but seemed intent on closing the gap between them.

Forcing out another burst of speed, she widened the gap momentarily, but the advantage was short lived. The man, judging from the heavy sound of his footfalls, closed the space between them again.

Shooting through a gap in the trees, Sabrina ran for the open area of the park. Faking a cramp, she gripped her side before stumbling to a stop. Bent forward, her elbows braced on her knees, she took deep breaths. Her arms dangled loosely, waiting for the man behind her to make an appearance. He burst through the trees, continued on the trail without even a glance in her direction.

He ran past, not more than twenty feet away from her. Eyeing him, she took in his black track pants and white muscle shirt. Extensive ink work decorated his shoulder and bicep. The Celtic design was distinctive.

His hair was dark, cut shorter than she remembered and his face was leaner, harder than it had been the last time she'd seen him. His name was Michael. They'd grown up in the same small Texas town, gone to school together, attended the same church. Her heart was pounding so hard it hurt and her palms were suddenly slick with sweat.

They'd never known each other well but he'd always stared at her a little too long, gotten a little too quiet when she was around. He'd always made her uncomfortable but seeing him now scared the shit out of her.

Every instinct Sabrina had was screaming, telling her she was in danger, urging her to run. He didn't appear by accident. This wasn't a coincidence.

Michael knew exactly who she was and he'd come here for her.

THE SABRINA VAUGHN SERIES

WAITING IN DARKNESS

CARVED IN DARKNESS

SACRIFICIAL MUSE

PROMISES TO KEEP

BLOOD OF SAINTS

(Available August, 2016 by Midnight Ink)

ABOUT THE AUTHOR

Maegan Beaumont is the author of the award-winning Sabrina Vaughn thriller series. Her debut novel, CARVED IN DARKNESS, was awarded the 2013 gold medal by Independent Publishers for outstanding thriller as well as being named a Forward, book of the year finalist and Debut novel of the year by Suspense Magazine. When she isn't locked in her office, torturing her protagonists, she's busy chasing chickens (and kids), hanging laundry and burning dinner. Either way, she is almost always in the company of her seven dogs, her truest and most faithful companions and her almost as faithful husband, Joe. Look for the fourth novel in her series, BLOOD OF SAINTS in August, 2016.

60878536R00135

Made in the USA
Columbia, SC
18 June 2019